That Ghoul Ava

The Queen of The Zombies

TW Brown

Portland, Oregon, USA

For the REAL Ava

A moment with the author…

Todd, what the hell are you thinking?

I have been asked that a few times over the years. Most recently it has been because of this very book. This is nothing like what people who read my stuff are used to in any way shape or form. Readers of my zombie stuff have come to expect certain things from me over the years. And let's not even bring up the *Dakota* series.

Still, this started out as an idea of doing something nice for a fan. There is a person who goes by 'That Ghoul Ava' on Twitter and some of the other social media outlets. She was one of my very first fans and extremely encouraging early on when I was lucky to sell a dozen books in a month. I wrote a short story for her as a way of saying thanks. The funny thing is, I really had a great time writing Ava.

Ava is meant to be funny. That is a tricky slope to climb in the world of writing. What you might think is hilarious, somebody else might not…or more often and likely, become offended. Ava will probably offend people. However, much like her namesake…she (and by extension, me) could care less.

If you are delicate or sensitive, if you think shows like *South Park* are unacceptable and don't belong on the air…then this is not the book for you. Given the chance, Ava would likely quote Jessica Rabbit with just a slight modification. "I'm not bad, I'm just written that way."

I realize that a lot of people don't read these introductions. Mostly they are for the writer to pat himself and a few people that you have never heard of on the back. So no doubt there will be a few reviews that call this infantile and offensive. Yeah, but the rest of you that read this and chuckle a few times…you are my audience anyways, not those wet blankets.

A few thanks are in order. Erin Sistak, the real ghoul; to Celia Aurora de Blas, the voice of Ava in the audio version…she is a-freakin'-mazing!; in addition, all the usual cast of characters that lend their support when I am questioning my choices in life…without you I could not do what I love for a living; most notably and important, my wife, Denise.

Last, this book was written during NaNoWriMo 2012. For those who are not tuned into such things, it is an annual event where the goal is to write a minimum of 50,000 words in a month. While I write almost every single day, there is something special about NaNoWriMo. The organization actually works to instill the love of writing in the younger generation. Check them out. Perhaps you can find a way that you can help keep this amazing program up and running.

This final paragraph is all about being selfish, so feel free to skip it. As a writer, you often work in a bit of a void. It is a solitary profession. My joy comes from hearing from the readers. The first thing I do in the morning when I sit down at my desk is to check my emails. Then, I pop over to my author page on Amazon and see if there are any new reviews on any of my titles. Reviews actually increase the visibility of a book and are welcome. Good or bad, I do read them. Very often I will try to express sincere thanks for their having taken the time in any case. So if you are so inclined, I hope that you will take the time to share your thoughts.

Take me…any way you want me…
TW Brown
November 2012

Contents

1

Same Ol' Situation

"Do you have to play this crap so loud?" Lisa said with that petulance that only teen girls can truly master. It's so sad. When we get older it just comes off as whiny or bitchy.

I pretended not to hear her. Not one thing that she could say or do was going to ruin my mood tonight. I was behind the wheel of my very first brand new car. No little tushies had planted themselves in this seat but mine. I had been assured that I was the very first person to test drive this little baby: A candy-apple red 2013 Corvette.

Now I'm not one of those girls who knows a lot about cars, so most of what the very cute salesman said just didn't stick. I think he even had a fancy name for the color red that my car was painted. Don't care.

I flew down the on-ramp that deposited me onto I-5 and went through the gears like I imagine those racecar drivers did when they zoomed around in circles. By the time I actually hit the freeway, I was on the high side of ninety miles per hour.

"Got your seatbelt on?" I asked. I wasn't planning on getting into a wreck…but who did? Safety first!

"Try to remember that only one of us is guaranteed not to die if you wreck this thing," Lisa yelled over the strains of the

1

luscious Brett Michaels who was currently begging me to talk dirty to him. Trust me when I tell you, *that* would be the least of his worries.

She was referring to the fact that I am a ghoul. Now let me assure you, being a ghoul is absolutely nothing like being a zombie. As if. Zombies are nasty creatures that eat the living. I only eat the dead. See? Big difference.

Lisa Jenkins was a teenage runaway. However, I doubted that her parents would come looking for her any time soon. In the six months that she had lived with me, I learned enough to know that it was unlikely that they were even aware that she had left home. Her father was long gone, and her single mother was busy sleeping with every bus boy, waiter, and bartender at this dirty little all-night place in Southeast Portland.

I'd popped in once and the woman was letting some slob put his hands up her skirt every time she came to the table. When she brought the actual meal to the table and cleared away the five empty beer bottles to make room, I almost lost my proverbial lunch. It was fried chicken, and I know for a fact that he didn't wash his hands before picking up that drumstick. And considering where that hand had just been...

But back to my dear friend and boon companion. (I don't actually know what a 'boon companion' is, but I heard that term used on some show on the local Public Broadcasting channel where everybody spoke with English accents. It sounded smart, so I claimed it.) I met Lisa one night shortly after my transformation. She had been in a seedy hotel after just giving birth. Her "boyfriend"—a pervy forty-something that actually convinced her to dump the child in the garbage right after giving birth—made the mistake of answering the door when I knocked. Long story short, baby was rescued and eventually given a home, perv was killed *and then* eaten, and Lisa became my roommate.

It was around the time that I met Lisa when I was introduced to a whole part of society that most folks don't realize exists under their noses. Call it supernatural or whatever you like, but things like ghouls, and ghosts, and vampires—like that snarky little bitch Belinda Yates—exist.

Some have gone on to sustain themselves through books like the one you are reading right now. You see, the best way to hide is in plain sight. You'd be surprised if I told you which of the other books in your collection are real; or at least based on real events in the lives of some of my fellow monsters. Yeah, most of them don't like the "M" word, but I like to consider myself a bit more progressive.

I actually decided to join the ranks of the writer-types after my first little "adventure" where I was hired to deal with a rogue vampire that had designs on the aforementioned Belinda. Well...not really Belinda, more specifically, her Kiss. (A "Kiss" for the uninitiated is what vampires call their little groups or clubs...whatever.) I didn't actually have to write, but Lisa thought it would be fun. She worries about the finances like nobody I have ever met and keeps telling me that the payday I got for taking care of Belinda's "little problem" won't last forever.

After I saw this car, I finally agreed that we needed an additional source of income. The only problem now was waiting for the next "job" from Morgan. For those of you who didn't catch my first little attempt at telling a story, Morgan is the psychic for my region. Unlike the ones on television that lie about being able to tell your future, Morgan is for real. Apparently true psychics are able to detect any supernaturals in their district. I don't know all of the details—mostly because she tells me very little—but I guess they act as some sort of mediator and boss for their given district.

The day I became a ghoul, I received a visit from Morgan. She kind of told me the rules. Mostly she went on about all the stuff I couldn't do. Of course, it was good old Ava's door that they knocked on when that vampire came in and started mucking things up.

By the time Billy Idol had told me all about what a great day it would be for a *White Wedding*, and the Go-Gos encouraged me to take a *Vacation*, we were home. And here was the reason we needed Morgan to show up with another job...or people needed to start buying these books. Home was no longer the dirty little apartment that I'd rented while I was a busty waitress with raven-black hair. Now we lived in a sweet little two-story looking down on Lake Oswego. (I never knew there was actually a lake here! Just thought it was a cute name for a town.)

It has four bedrooms! Now I wasn't ever going to hear the pitter-patter of ghoulish feet, but maybe Lisa might give it a go when she is actually old enough and meets a nice guy. I have a feeling that I will be living vicariously through her.

And there you have it—my word for the day: *vicariously.* Take that Morgan. She always talks to me like I am the idiot child. Well now that I have hired a ghost writer—literally, I seriously have this ghost that comes in and helps, she possesses Lisa when it is time to sit down and put the story together—I get to hear all sorts of big words.

Chantal, my ghostly pal, likes to chat sometimes during the day. She sometimes slips in to Lisa while she is dozing and will chat with me about stuff. At first it was weird having these conversations that Lisa has no memory of, and I have to get it straight who I am talking to or what I have said to Chantal-Lisa and what I have said to Lisa-Lisa.

Hmm, that reminds me. I fiddle with my iPod docking station and thumb to a song. One of my favorite features of this home was the sound system. You can have music—or whatever you are watching on television—piped throughout the whole place. *Head-to-Toe* by Lisa Lisa and the Cult Jam starts, and I head for the basement door.

"Back in a few minutes," I call over my shoulder. I catch Lisa's face in the reflection of the kitchen window. Her nose wrinkles. If I wasn't so secure in our friendship, my feelings might be hurt. Hey…a girl's gotta eat.

My basement is the other feature that really sold this house to me. A serial killer would blow his…well, whatever it is that they blow. You can bet my basement would be the thing that would send said serial killer over the edge.

It is absolutely sound proof. I tested it out early when I brought my ex-husband's guitar amplifier down here. My actual goal was to check out the real estate agent's claim that this basement was, in fact, sound proof. If I just happened to blow up his amplifier in the process, that would be icing on the cake.

I plugged in the pretty green guitar that was still in my closet despite the fact that we had been divorced long enough for that cheating bastard to remarry and have a pair of twin snot factories...err...I mean a lovely set of boy and girl twins. (I can never remember which is fraternal and which is maternal...not like I actually care.) Anyways, I plugged that guitar in, turned every single knob on the amplifier to "10" and strummed. I forgot all about my super-sensitive ghoul hearing.

For almost a week I was absolutely deaf. Thankfully I have the ability to heal. Supposedly, I can take a shotgun blast to the chest and not die. I'd just as soon not test the theory, but it is kind of nice to think that that little bit of insurance is in my tool box. To actually kill me, you need to either sever my head, or pierce my heart with a weapon made from cold-treated iron— whatever the heck that is. I feel comfortable sharing that with you because you will either dismiss this as just another one of "those" stories that are so popular right now, or you just won't ever feel the need to go out and hunt down a ghoul that is trying to make the world a better place.

So once I could hear again, Lisa assured me that she did not actually hear a thing. She was really glad when my hearing came back. I guess I am one of those women with a naturally loud voice.

So back to my basement. As I told you, I am a ghoul. I eat the dead. To be clear, they have to be "unprocessed." I don't know if you are aware of what they do to a person before spray painting them and stuffing them in a box, but no ghoul would ever touch a body after a mortician got ahold of it. I keep about a half dozen corpses on ice for those times when I can't go out and hunt down a fresh meal.

This is another of the perks from that job I did for Belinda-the-vampire-bitch. She occasionally has one of her minions bring by a thrall that might have been snacked on a bit too heavily or the chance human version of a monster that they might stumble across. I had no idea that so many icky beasties maintain human form and transform under whatever weird circumstance is their trigger: full moons, high tides, the opening day of football season.

Opening the walk-in refrigerator, I pull the first body out and set him on the huge table. Already the smell is causing my mouth to water. I know it will just be a moment—

"Mrrgl."

Oh yeah. Sharkmouth makes the scene and I dig in. I can't really explain it better than that. When I smell a dead body—something that you would probably find repulsive—it is like being in Martha Stewart's kitchen on Thanksgiving. The smell is beyond delicious.

My mouth does this thing that sort of defies biology. It stretches out several inches and these three razor-sharp rows of needle-like fangs drop. I become the human equivalent of one of those wood chipper thingies. I can down a whole body in less than ten minutes. The only part that is a bit icky for me is regurging up the clothes. To my credit, I strip the bodies that are put in my fridge. However, I don't exactly have control over my appetite. When I encounter a dead body out and about, I just can't help myself.

The best thing I can equate it to is what used to happen with those spray cans of whip cream. I couldn't open my fridge when one of those things were in there back when I was alive without grabbing it, popping the top, and shooting a mouthful of tasty, sweet whipped cream into my mouth.

So anyways, I got my Sharkmouth going, and made short work of my dinner. I think we found this one under a bridge. Probably not the solution to the homeless situation that they were thinking of with *Comic Relief*; but, in my defense, he was already dead. Being out in the elements is really not something that we are designed for in our human form.

When I was finished, I went back upstairs. Lisa was already asleep. She was sprawled on the couch, the remote slipping from her fingers. I glanced at the screen long enough to decide that if I ever got the chance, I might break my rule about eating a live human if I ever met the 'Sham Wow' guy. I turned off the idiot box and pulled the blanket that was draped over the back of the sofa across Lisa and headed upstairs.

My room is a marvel. It has shutters that allow in absolutely no sunlight. That way I didn't have to stay in a rickety closet like I did back in the apartment. One of the drawbacks of being a ghoul is the vampire-like aversion to sunlight. For some reason, it burns like acid if it touches my tender, gray skin. (Although I do keep it airbrushed a golden bronze most times when we are going out in public.)

"Is this your idea of living a low key life?" a familiar voice whispered from the darkness.

I did my best not to shriek. However, I have this thing that happens when I get scared. My toenails and fingernails turn to three-inch claws. I've ruined more shoes in the past several months...

"Morgan, I wish you wouldn't do that," I managed to say. Sometimes I went all sharkmouth, too, depending on how scared I got.

So that brings me to another of my abilities. I can totally see in the dark. And not Paris Hylton sex-tape vision. I can *see* in the dark like a normal person can in the daylight. However, for some strange reason, Morgan is invisible to me when she chooses. It is like she wraps herself in the darkness and vanishes. Also, I can hear. I'm talking footsteps of a fly on the other side of the wall type stuff. It is like having a radio tuner in my head. I just scan the area, and I can pick up on things as far as a few blocks away. (I know this because Lisa and I played this game one night where she kept walking and talking in a whisper until I couldn't hear her.) However, like her ability to evade my sight, Morgan can also be so quiet that I can't hear her so much as breathe. (And she does, because I watched her chest one time to see if it rose and fell...it did.)

"And I will remind you that I am the authority in these parts and keep my own council."

Bitchy mood, I thought. *Great, just what I need.* What I said was, "So what brings you to my house tonight? I know it isn't to hang out and do each other's hair and nails." To emphasize my point, I kicked off my newest pair of ruined Nikes.

"It seems that there has been a disturbance." Morgan moved into view. Now when I say that, what I mean is that she went from being invisible to standing three feet away from me in the blink of an eye.

"In the Force?" I scoffed and sat on the edge of my bed to pull my shredded socks off my feet. Bummer, these were the ones with the cute little roses on the toes. I kind of liked those socks.

"Your attempts at humor have not gotten any better." Morgan walked to my door and pulled it shut.

"Neither has your attitude," I shot back. "You sent me on a job with the high likelihood that I would die, but that I would do enough damage so your precious little vampire could come in and finish the job."

"Not true," Morgan countered. "We gave you a fifty-fifty chance."

"You still sent me in underprepared and with the thought that my death would be an acceptable loss."

"We paid you very handsomely for your services." Morgan gave me a dismissive wave. I wondered, and not for the first time, if I could take her in a fight.

"Lot of good that would have done me if I were dead."

"You *are* dead."

I have no idea how long I stood there with my mouth open. I desperately wanted to fire off a witty comeback. Sadly, that is not really my strong suit. Instead, I went to what I felt I did best. I glared.

"I suppose you came here with a purpose?" I finally said after a few seconds of uncomfortable silence that was probably worse on me than on the emotionally stunted Morgan.

"I have." Morgan took a seat in the over-stuffed easy chair. She settled in and went so far as to grab the handle on the side and recline! Talk about making yourself comfortable. "There has been an incident just outside of the city in a little town called Estacada."

I had grown up in the Portland area. There are several little towns on the fringe that are mostly full of loggers, and, as of late, meth cooks. Back in the Seventies, there were always stories of people growing marijuana out in the forests. Supposedly they had the farms booby-trapped and if they caught trespassers, they just killed them and left the body for the animals. It was the Pacific Northwest's equivalent to moonshining, I guess. If you believe the stories, that is.

"When you say incident..." I let that hang in the air and become my question.

"I have been..." Morgan paused. For just a second, I thought I saw something flit across her face that *almost* looked like an emotion. Seriously, this lady could make Mr. Spock look like a Jerry Springer guest when it came to containing emotional expression. "I have been *informed* that there may be zombies in the woods."

I looked at Morgan, and then I pulled out my phone and tapped the screen to wake it up. Yep, it was the middle of March. That would rule out April Fool's. I tucked my phone away.

"Zombies?" I tried not to sound like I thought she was full of it, but I'm not sure how well I managed to hide my skepticism. "Like *Dawn of the Dead* zombies, or like *Serpent and the Rainbow* zombies?"

I was so proud of myself. I was never into the whole scary movie kick when I was human. Honestly, I was a giant scairdy cat. Those sorts of things gave me nightmares. Now, heck, I'd done battle with an honest-to-goodness vampire. I'd spoken to a few ghosts, and I live with a teenage girl. Movie monsters had nothing on my reality. Since Morgan had let it slip that a lot of what most people would consider popular fiction had some basis in reality, I decided that I would do some homework. Turns out Lisa was a big fan of the stuff. So I let her pick the selections for movie night.

"We aren't sure yet," Morgan said with all seriousness.

"Wait! What?"

"There has only been one report and it was made by a witch that has a propensity for sipping a bit too much hemlock tea."

I was pretty sure that hemlock was some type of poison, but

I could worry about that later. Morgan was talking about zombies. Worse, when I asked what type, her answer leads me to believe that there is more than *one* type of zombie! That tops poison drinking witches in my book.

"So what am I supposed to do? Do I go out there with a shotgun and blow their brains out?" I said with as much of a laugh as I could muster.

"I imagine that would be one way to deal with the situation," Morgan said with her usual lack of emotion.

"You can't be serious."

"I am absolutely serious. Do I strike you as somebody who jokes?"

I tried to imagine Morgan even smiling and it gave me a bit of a chill. It would probably be like a shark's smile...the last thing you ever saw before you became a snack. There was something about this woman that was just the most pure form of scary. And she was a tiny little thing. And then it dawned on me who she reminded me of: Carol Kane in that Bill Murray movie, *Scrooged*. She was that ghost or fairy, or whatever the heck she was supposed to be. But when she hit Bill Murray with that toaster, I laughed so hard I think I peed my pants just a little bit. She even had a voice very similar to Ms. Kane. Of course I would never tell her that. The only reason that I am sharing it with you here is because I know that she will never stoop to reading any of my books.

"So what in the world would zombies be doing here? And what am I supposed to do if I find one?"

"If I had all of these answers, do you think that I would be here asking you to investigate? That is what you are going to be paid for, Ava."

"So am I supposed to just investigate, or am I supposed to kill something?"

"I imagine that will be determined once you go check things out," Morgan said with a sigh as she unreclined (is that even a word?) from the recliner and stood up. "Perhaps I have overestimated your abilities. Maybe I should find somebody else."

I thought about that last seven figure paycheck. Considering the fact that I had worked as a waitress, and a good night was when I walked out with a hundred bucks, I decided that I wouldn't have a problem taking a drive out to Estacada to look for zombies. My only concern was Lisa.

"You might want to leave your pet human at home," Morgan said.

I know she told me that she isn't a fortune teller or a mind reader, but that was just too spooky. I think she had a good point, though. If these were the *Dawn of the Dead*-type of zombie, I would feel just terrible if Lisa got bit and turned into one of those things. Of course that brought me to another question.

"How come this isn't ending up on the news? If there are zombies, wouldn't that be something that the humans would want to report?"

Morgan was silent for a moment. I think that worried me more than anything else. She was keeping something from me and I didn't like it one bit.

"Somebody is keeping the zombies under control for now," Morgan finally said.

Now I was even more confused. There was so much wrong with that sentence that I had no idea where to start. I decided to just wade in—not that I expected much in the way of answers.

"Some*body*?"

Morgan's face actually seemed to melt into something resembling an emotion for just a split second. At least I think so. It might have been a trick of the shadows or something, but I was almost positive that I saw one eyebrow knit ever so slightly.

"There may be a person behind this," Morgan admitted.

"So if it is a person..." My mind tried to make what I considered to be a logical jump. "Then it must be some sort of voodoo thing, right?"

I had to consider that voodoo was real. After all, just scroll back a bit to that whole part where I mentioned meeting vampires and ghosts. Oh yeah, and the part about me being a ghoul. So if those things were real, then why not voodoo?

"Not necessarily," Morgan said with a slight movement of her head that may have been a shake in the general direction of "no."

"But if somebody is in control…" I heard that sound in my voice that was dangerously close to a whine. This was not going to get me any answers. I took a second and regrouped. Maybe if I tackled something else.

"You said something about 'for now' when you said that these zombies are under control."

"Bravo for catching on," Morgan said. The only problem was that I was not sure if she was being sarcastic or not.

"Does that mean this might be some sort of beginning of one of those zombie apocalypse thingamajigs that everybody seems so excited to read about?"

Personally, I didn't get the whole infatuation with that genre. Anybody with half a brain would know that a zombie apocalypse would eventually mean that there would be no more *anything*! Things like hot showers and stuff would be gone. It would be like the camping trip that never ended. I don't know about you, but I like to maintain a certain degree of personal hygiene. Soaps would stop being made…and that would be the least of our problems. You think you have trouble with feminine itching…or the lack of "feeling fresh" now? Try living without the local drug store or supermarket.

And for you men…I wouldn't start feeling so smug just yet. There are certain things that a woman may or may not do in these modern times regarding "your little soldier" that I can promise would come to an immediate halt when you stop being able to keep that area clean.

I knew this one guy, and he was just so dreamy; broad chest, dazzling smile, and strong swimmer's legs that were attached to buns that you could bounce a dime off. We met one night in a little club downtown and I swear that he was so well-groomed that I was certain he had to be gay. When he whispered in my ear that he would like to buy me a drink, I had to go check my make-up.

I am a very busty gal with my 38DDs, and I play to my strengths. I also have Elvira-black hair that comes to my waist. If I get a bit too carried away with the make-up, apparently some people have suspected me of being a drag queen. Now I don't want to get into the whole thing about whether or not that is a bad thing. Let's just say that when that revelation was made to me a few years back, I learned to tone down the face paint.

Anyways, we get back to my place and he is one of those guys who likes to do a little bit of taste-testing before he gets down to business. *Yay for me!* is what I was thinking. Me being the kind of gal who is into reciprocity, I went to return the favor. I got to his naval when I noticed what I first believed to be just a case of bad feet. I was prepared to overlook that…until I got to the actual source of that sweaty stench.

So, fellas, if you think that whole zombie apocalypse thing is gonna just-freakin'-rock, let me tell you that there are some major downsides.

"…would take a lot more than that." Crap, Morgan had been saying something important. I knew that she was going to be annoyed, but I didn't have much to lose since she already thought I was an idiot.

"Excuse me?" I tried to make it sound like I wanted her to elaborate. She is far too smart for that.

"I should have known when you had that vapid look in your eyes that you were off on some sort of mental picnic," Morgan said. The thing is, she said it with as close to no emotion as possible. It was like my Speak-and-Spell using a female voice.

"Sorry, just trying to wrap my mind around how bad a zombie apocalypse would be."

"So you didn't hear a single word that I said." I couldn't swear to it, but it almost sounded like Morgan was annoyed.

"Okay, I'm listening." I even cupped my hands to my ears for effect.

"I said that all those books and movies are preposterous. Do you really think that one person infected with some sort of zombie virus could cause a chain reaction that would wipe out the world? It would take something a great deal more widespread."

Morgan headed for the door and started downstairs. I guess she was leaving. I followed her down and even edged around her to open the door. I doubted that it would raise my standing in her eyes, but perhaps a little politeness would gain me a little something.

"I want to repeat," Morgan turned and stood in my doorway, "that I believe it would be a very bad idea to take your little human pet with you on this assignment."

"She'd not a—" I began to protest, but she was gone. I could say that she vanished in the blink of an eye...but I hadn't blinked.

"What assignment?"

I jumped. If my heart still beat, it would have been pounding like a Rikki Rockett drum solo. Instead, my fingernails and toenails went switchblade. Lisa took a step back and had the decency to look apologetic. *How had she snuck up on me?* Hmm.

"Morgan just came by with a job." I shut the door and headed upstairs to my room. It would be daylight soon, I could feel it. "She thinks I can handle it by myself and didn't want you getting involved." I guess that was at least part of the truth. I wasn't all that sure that Morgan believed that I could handle anything by myself.

"What is the job?" Lisa moved past me into my room and plopped down on my bed. I could tell by the look on her face that she wasn't buying any of what I was selling.

"Just something up in Estacada. I will head there tonight and be back before morning most likely."

"So is it werewolves?" Lisa said that with way too much enthusiasm. I guess this was all just a big adventure to her. She still was not really in tune with the whole "we are monsters" part of things. If she knew how close she'd come to being a late-night snack to Belinda back when we first started hanging out together...perhaps she would be a little more concerned with her own safety.

"No." I closed my bedroom door. A little bit of dim gray light was starting to spill across the floor of my hallway.

"Then maybe you can let me know what it is, and *I* can decide if it is too dangerous for me or not." Lisa folded her arms across her chest and cocked one hip. That was teenage girl body language for 'I ain't budging until you talk.'

"Zombies," I said.

Seriously, what could it hurt? In fact, we'd watched a bunch of those movies. Even went to some author's book signing. Marvin, or Mark, or Mel Tufo…something like that—he had some series that she was just crazy about. She got home that night and wrapped the book in plastic like it was a priceless artifact. I was certain that when I told her it might be zombies that she would see the logic in sitting this one out. After all, I am a ghoul. I was pretty sure I am off the menu.

I could not have been more wrong.

2

Rumors in the Air

Lisa was at my door within minutes of sunset. Lucky for her that I wasn't busy. Hey, I might be a ghoul, but I still have my needs. I had done some searches on Google about zombies—the real ones...not the movie versions. I figured I knew all that I needed to deal with the made-in-Hollywood kind—a bullet to the head or whatever.

In a day's worth of research, I came up with salt. Now what you did with the salt depended on what you read. I could make a circle with it. I could throw it on the zombie—that one seemed like a last ditch tactic. I was pretty sure that if it came to that, I was already in big trouble.

"Can I drive?" Lisa asked, twirling the keys on her finger.

"The Corvette?" I had to stifle a laugh. Hadn't she just been going on yesterday about my frivolous spending?

"Did you get another car when I wasn't paying attention?"

"You can drive, but if you so much as get too many bugs on the windshield...it is game over."

Lisa let out a squeal that could almost cause an ear hemorrhage and raced down the stairs. I am pretty sure the only things capable of hearing in that register were ghouls and dogs. I grabbed my plastic bag from the grocery store with a variety of salts. I had the one with the little girl and the umbrella, the generic store brand, and then, as an added bonus, I'd had Lisa get a

17

thing of sea salt. Hey, no such thing as being over-prepared when it comes to dealing with zombies. Now there is something I never imagined in a million years I would have to say with any sort of seriousness.

We pulled out of the driveway. That is how long it took me to regret letting Lisa drive. First, I was thrown forward hard enough that I was pretty sure I was going to have whiplash (if ghouls can get whiplash, that is). Then, I was slammed back in my seat hard enough that, if this would have been a cartoon, my teeth would still be floating in the air where my head used to be.

Then she turned on the stereo.

Apparently the little delinquent had been planning on my saying yes. She already had her iPod docked and a song queued up. Now when I was young...err...young*er*...groups like Pantera were considered pretty extreme. I listened to them when I wanted to piss off my folks. I didn't even like them that much. Megadeth and Metallica fell into that grouping as well. Well, Metallica did until they went emo-metal with *Nothing Else Matters*.

The stuff screaming out of my speakers had absolutely no relation to actual music. I get that each generation thinks theirs is the one that cornered the market. With my folks it was Elvis, The Beatles, and Barbara Streisand. How you can link those together is anybody's guess. My mom cried when John Lennon got shot. I cried when Poison broke up. To each his or her own, I guess. Still, this noise was absolutely ridiculous. If you shoved a microphone down some guy's throat and then slammed his testicles in a sliding glass door, he would probably be more musical than this garbage.

I endured it for all of ten minutes. Say what you will, but I am proud that I lasted that long. A moment later, we were back on the road and heading towards Estacada. I swapped out her iPod for mine and was soon just a bit envious of Katrina and her ability to walk on sunshine. Lisa seemed unimpressed.

We drove in silence for a while, but I could almost feel the pressure dropping as a storm moved in steadily. As we turned on to a stretch of highway that ran in a series of lazy curves beside some river or another—don't ask me which one the damn things are everywhere in this state...and then there is the whole 'Is it a river or a stream" thing. How should I know, and why do I care? It is moving water and you can skip rocks across it. Beyond that...is there really a difference? Anyway...it started to rain.

"Why is *your* stuff music and *my* stuff crap?" Lisa grumbled. *Ah yes, the leading edge of another storm had arrived.*

"I never said any such thing," I replied, knowing very well that an answer like that would not divert or lessen the coming storm.

One thing about being a ghoul, I do have a rather extreme sense of smell. Lisa was being paid a visit by Aunt Scarlet. I have heard some people say that PMS is a construct of the female psyche. Funny how most of those "experts" happen to be men.

"You don't have to say it. Every time I put on my music, you either make a face or turn it off."

"Look, when you get your car, and I have to ride in it, you can play your music to your little heart's content."

In my mind, I was slapping my forehead. Hadn't my own mother said that exact same thing to me when I was close to around Lisa's age? And those words had come back to bite her in the ass.

My senior year in high school, she had gone to Arizona to visit her mom and dad—my grandma and granddaddy. Guess who had to pick her up at the airport when she came home? And I was driving my beat up Toyota Corolla with a Kenwood stereo and hundred watt amp (that was probably worth more than the car)—ah, the Eighties. So, at the time, I was dating this guy named Joel. He was a big Van Halen fan. I hadn't really gotten into them yet. I was still listening to the Top Forty.

I credit Joel for really getting me started in the rock music. He took me to my first concert. It was Scorpions, Iron Maiden and Girl's School. It was better than sex. Well, it was better than high school sex, but that is a topic for another time.

Anyways, so I go to pick up my mom. In my cassette deck is the first (and best in my opinion) Van Halen tape. I may or may not have sat in the parking lot for a few extra moments fast forwarding to a specific spot on the tape. Say what you want about your CDs, and various digital music players, there was something magic about those days of having a small suitcase of cassette tapes in your back seat.

We got my mom's bags and threw them in the back seat, then once we both had on our seatbelts...I turned the ignition. When those first few bangs on the drum sounded...and then Eddie Van Halen tore into *Eruption* like I do a dead wino, my mom just about gave me a sunroof. As I backed out of the space, she started yelling about turning off 'that infernal racket!'

"When we drive your car, you can play your music," I parroted a saying that she had used on me since I was about four.

"Look," I glanced at Lisa and tried my best to smile, "how about you ease me into your stuff. I'm sure you listen to something that doesn't sound like somebody caught their testicles in a garbage disposal."

Lisa actually had the nerve to appear to be *considering* my offer! I was about to take it back, after all...it is *my* car!

"Fine," she agreed. "I have a few other bands I can probably listen to that you won't hate."

"And if something of mine is just too much, then you let me know. I will try and keep it fair." I was feeling pretty good about myself. My mother never would have made such a compromise.

"This," Lisa said, and then made a choking, gagging sound while clutching her throat.

"What?" At this very moment, Steve Perry and the boys were urging me not to stop believin'. How could anybody have a problem with Journey?

"Reminds me of that stupid show, *Glee*." Lisa held her nose and waved one hand in front of her face. I saw her point. Maybe later I would try to sneak in some *Wheel in the Sky* or *Lights*.

I thumbed ahead and introduced her to Dexy's Midnight Runners. She seemed to hate them considerably less than Journey. We drove along the rest of the way in relative peace. I even grabbed her a four-pack of peanut butter cups when I stopped for gas. I don't care what any doctor says, but when Aunt Flo stops by, chocolate is the answer.

Eventually we rolled into what was considered the main drag in Estacada. No surprise, it was called Main Street. I pulled in to a little strip mall with a pizza place and a coin-operated laundry. At the moment, there were more people in the laundry. Sunglasses on—my eyes are black, not just the pretty part either...the entire eyeball was entirely black which tended to unnerve some folks—I hopped out of the car and strolled into the laundry.

"So do we just start asking?" Lisa whispered.

I glanced at her, and that was when it hit me. I didn't have a plan. I had no clue what to do. Maybe zombies were like vampires. As a ghoul, I can smell a dead body from a pretty fair distance. They smell like the best thing you can imagine. Think pumpkin pie and chocolate chip cookies. However, vampires smell disgusting to me. The best thing I can compare it to is maybe chocolate cake frosted in Dumpster filth and dipped in sewage. I haven't gotten around to asking why yet. I'm not sure if Morgan would know...or care.

I briefly considered calling her up and asking, but I knew that nothing good would come of that. I decided that I didn't need her. In fact, within just a matter of seconds, I had managed to turn the entire situation around and had myself convinced that the reason that Morgan had given me this job is because she had no clue. I was her only hope.

I was about to head inside the pizza place when I caught a whiff of something. Have you ever visited a place that makes candy? Specifically, a place that makes all types of fudge and chocolate treats? That first blast of cocoa-scented air is magical. I used to go to this place in the Pearl District when I wanted to pretend that I was an affluent young woman. I always had my cover blown the moment I engaged in a conversation with somebody who was actually *from* the Pearl District. I didn't know anything about art or what the latest must-read book happened to be at the moment. And Heaven forbid my phone ring. As soon as I pulled out my pay-by-the-month model with absolutely no special features...so busted.

Back to what I was saying before I got sidetracked…

This smell hit my nose and I am pretty sure I had a tiny orgasm. My knees almost folded up like a lawn chair. But then I caught a whiff of something else. It was just below the surface of that other smell, and I had to concentrate because I began to think that I'd imagined it. It was like my mind had decided that nothing could smell that good and so it had popped the bubble by creating this other smell.

The more I tried to focus on it, the more it seemed to stay just out of reach. I turned back to the street and looked around. A few cars passed, but there was nobody on the street. That seemed wrong somehow. After all, it was Friday night and school was within a week or so of letting out for summer break. If nothing else, there should have at least been a few juvenile delinquents out prowling and working up the courage to cause trouble.

I tried to home back in on that wonderful smell, but it had gone away as if it never had existed. Hmm…maybe it hadn't. But no, my body physically reacted to that smell. It was real, and now I needed to track it down, because the only thing that has that sort of smell for me is something dead.

"Did you see that lady?" Lisa tugged at my arm, snapping me out of my little aroma-induced trance.

"Huh?" That should have been an obvious enough response for Lisa to be able to deduce my answer. However, Lisa often misses the obvious.

"That lady that just walked into that pizza place?"

"No, but what about her?"

"She was…" Lisa stood there with her mouth open. It was like she completely switched off. The last time she did that…

The smell hit me at the same time as I heard that voice. "Morgan told me that I would find you here."

"Belinda." I tried not to make that one word sound at all how I felt about the person in question. "What brings you out here to the sticks?"

"I have a thrall out here," she said as she stepped from the shadows and sort of oozed behind Lisa, running her fingers along my friend's shoulder.

22

The thing you need to know about Belinda is that she was turned a few hundred years ago. She was obviously young, and now she uses that to her advantage. She dresses like jail bait and apparently has a thing for dirty old men. Her hair is blonde enough to almost be white and her blue eyes remind me of this baby doll I had as a little girl. They sparkle, but there is no life in them at all.

Tonight she was wearing shorts...almost. I mean I am sure that they started off as shorts, but I just can't see anybody modifying them to the extent that they have so many tiny rips in them located with such strategic perfection that they come very close to making her a flasher. And the bare midriff tee shirt looks to be a size or two small...at least for her bra-less boobs. It sports the Estacada High School Rangers' logo, albeit somewhat stretched and malformed by the pair of unfairly firm mounds stuffed under it.

"What, dare I ask, exactly is a thrall?" I decided to play along and play nice for now.

"My need to feed is not something I can always find a source to quench. For just such occasions, I have a few humans that give willingly."

"So you are here for the cuisine," I said with a laugh that I hoped sounded pleasant and not too mocking.

"In a manner of speaking," Belinda agreed. "But I actually wanted to find you first."

My warning bells went off. There was no universe where Belinda and I could be friends. She was rude and overbearing and thought she was God's gift. Plus, her body was frozen in the form of a girl in her late teens which was so damn unfair. I mean, if I'd been transformed into a ghoul when I was her age and could walk around without *my* bra...then maybe...

"Focus, Ava," Belinda snapped her fingers in front of my face.

"Sorry, just considering the likelihood of anything you say being anything that I want to hear."

"Actually, I wanted to let you know that one of my Kiss saw what he was certain had to be a zombie, but if you are going to be your typical—"

"Wait," I cut her off. "So one of your vampire minions saw an actual zombie?"

"That is the thing…he wasn't sure what it was until Morgan paid a visit and issued a warning that we should stay clear of the area."

"Can zombies hurt vampires?" I asked. Honestly…I didn't know and needed as much information as possible.

"Doubtful," Belinda said.

That is when it dawned on me…she didn't know! She was not here to pass on any information, she was here because there was something going on and she didn't know anything about it! I only had a moment to wonder if this was that OCD-level curiosity that vampires supposedly possessed.

"Well then, what is it that you want?"

Belinda was silent. That was perhaps the most peculiar thing. She was never at a loss for words. I was getting nervous. There were a lot of differences between her and me, so help was the last thing that I would expect.

"If I tell you this," Belinda started, her lips curled up into what I was almost sure had to be an equivalent of a smile, "then you and I are even. I owe you nothing."

Okay? Now I was really at a loss. What was she talking about? The only real interaction we'd had was when that vampire had come in to her territory and I'd been tasked to kill him. But I'd been paid. A lot.

"I know that you are clueless, but you would eventually find out and then it would be even worse."

Nope. Still not getting it. I wish she didn't have Lisa all tranced out. I bet she would be pretty helpful right now. She knows all this crap. However, she was still standing there with her mouth open and a single strand of drool starting to trickle out of one side.

"You performed a favor for me," Belinda stated. She said this like it was a complete explanation that made everything clear.

When I just stood there, she made a low growl in her throat

24

and her eyes did this flashing thing. It was weirder because her face did not change. Not a wrinkle of the brow, not a turning down of the lips. Nothing.

"By the laws of the Kiss, any who do a service that are not a part of the Kiss must either be offered a place amongst us or be the recipient of a favor. Since there is absolutely no way that you can become one of us in your...*condition* (she said that word like it tasted bad coming out of her mouth), then I offer you some information that may be of great service to you."

"And when you give me this information that is so important, but that Morgan just happened to leave out, then we are even?" That seemed like a risky proposition. What if the information was bogus, or what if it provided me with absolutely nothing useful?

"This information will be of great assistance, and I can promise you that Morgan was not aware," Belinda said as if she could read my thoughts. "If she knew this then she might not have enlisted *you*. She might have gone outside her district for a professional."

I wanted to be offended, but the reality was that I was absolutely an amateur. Heck, the only knowledge that I was armed with up to this point had come from Google. I seriously doubted that they were the authority when it comes to the *real* supernatural world.

"And if I agree, then you tell me and...what?"

"Nothing," Belinda said. This was not the first time that I cursed her visible lack of emotion. If that girl ever took an interest in poker, the card sharks of the world were in for a mess of trouble.

"Can you be just a bit more clear?" I finally asked when it was obvious that she was done with her explanation.

"*Nothing* is fairly self-explanatory. However, since I am aware of your intellectual short-comings, I will provide some clarity. What I am going to tell you is vital to your ability to handle this situation. As far as providing you with anything concrete? I doubt it, considering that what I am about to tell you has never been more than simple speculation for hundreds of years."

"Okay." Now don't mistake my one word response for simple approval. That word probably took at least five seconds to say. If I wrote it out the way it came from my mouth, it would have taken at least two lines. I just think that looks silly whenever I have read a book and the writer uses six O's, five H's, a single K, a dozen A's and three Y's. There was a lot of mixed emotion behind my response. Unfortunately, vampires do not have the market cornered when it comes to curiosity. Avas hold their own in that department.

"You may be dealing with The Queen of the Zombies."

I have no idea how long that sentence hung in the air, but I do know that I stood there with my mouth open like my friend Lisa for quite a while.

Then I started laughing.

"I am glad you find that amusing, but I doubt that you realize just how serious this situation could be if that is a fact instead of just a rumor," Belinda said. Now, once again, there was very little change in her expression, but she was definitely scolding me. However, there was something else there, and if I was right…this was no laughing matter.

"Okay, so let's say that this queen of the zombies (I had not yet learned to respect or fear her enough to speak with capital letters) is here. What's the big deal?"

"Since I am pressed for time, I will dispense with asking you what you know about world history between around 1340 and 1350. I know you have to at least have heard about The Black Death."

"That plague thingy that wiped everybody out?" *Ha! I'm not so dumb.*

"If it had 'wiped everybody out' as you so eloquently put it, we would not be having this conversation," Belinda said. I really hated how much she enjoyed putting me in what she considered to be my place.

"Fine, but didn't it kill over half the people in Europe or something?"

"Very close," Belinda said, surprising me with a confirmation that my SWAG (Silly-Wild-Ass-Guess) was on target…or at least in the general area. "However, it was the Augustines and the Templars who created that version of history to be passed on."

"Huh?" Back to being the stupid girl.

"I'm sure that you have at least heard about the Templars. Plenty of movies have used them in some manner or another as bad guys."

I just gave a nod. I didn't think that another really long 'okay' was appropriate. Belinda looked around almost like she was concerned that somebody could sneak up on us. Trust me, if something could…I didn't want to meet it.

"The Queen of the Zombies came to power and tried to take the world," Belinda said. "It took the combined efforts of the Templars and the Augustines to ensure that the history books said otherwise. In fact, it was the Augustines that convinced Giovanni Boccaccio to write *The Decameron*."

When I just stared blankly, she went on with her explanation. It wasn't that I didn't believe her; I was actually trying to figure out what the hell *The Decameron* might be.

"Supposedly she was imprisoned in the same secret lair where Arthur's sword, the Arc of the Covenant, and the Christ's drinking goblet are secured."

Now it was just starting to sound like a bad *Indiana Jones* rip off. Still, as smart as she *might* be, I didn't credit Belinda with the ability to make all of this up in the fly.

"So how do I kill her?" That seemed like a pretty logical question. And considering all of the stuff that she seemed to know about this so-called queen of zombies (notice how I left of the word 'the'?), it did not seem a stretch that she might know.

"I don't think you can."

Well that was not at all the answer I had hoped for. Besides, every monster has a way to kill it. Right? I mean, if you go by the movies—which supposedly have some basis in fact according Morgan—then it would stand to reason that every monster has an Achilles Heel.

"I believe that those who managed to lock her away would have killed her if given the chance. After all, she was trying to subjugate the entire world and managed something almost sin-gle-handedly that even nations marching under their silly little banners have not accomplished—the death of over half the population of the civilized world." Belinda flashed her fangs in what I thought was a yawn...until she snarled. "My thrall!"

And just that quick, she was gone.

"...standing right over there," Lisa said. She sounded like a record getting up to speed.

I gave her a curious look. I had no idea how Belinda did it, but I know I didn't like it. The way she could just pop in and put Lisa into what was basically a coma for an indeterminate time, and then pop out and let her return with absolutely zero knowledge as to what had happened.

"Who was?" And that was the other problem. I couldn't re-call what the heck she was talking about.

"This lady..." Lisa drifted off for a second. I looked around expecting Belinda to be back, but then she snapped out of it and continued. "It was weird because I almost thought she wasn't real. Nobody stands that still. Plus, it was like there was not even a hint of this soft evening breeze causing anything to ruffle. And she has dark hair that should have been waving at least a little bit."

My mind seemed to fizzle for a second. There was some-thing else that had been happening right around that moment. Now I couldn't remember. I know I'm not the brightest girl, but I'm not stupid. I focused my attention on trying to remember exactly what had been happening when Belinda so rudely inter-rupted. I could remember getting out of the car...walking up to the coin-op laundry, and then thinking that maybe we should look in the pizza place. I was sure I was missing something.

3

Nobody's Fool

"You sure are acting weird," Lisa said with what sounded like genuine concern.

Of course, a lot of that had to do with the way that I had literally scooped her up in my arms and dumped her in the Corvette. I had jumped over my car—I didn't actually know I could do such a thing until that very minute—climbed in, and took off like I'd stolen something. Oh yeah…and I couldn't get my finger- or toenails to retract or my sharkmouth to pull back.

"Mrgll shrmf."

What was the use? There would be no way for her to understand me until I could dial my feelings back a little. I had plenty of things to be concerned about, but at the moment, I couldn't whittle my list down.

I briefly wondered if there would ever be a time when I would not be having some massive revelation dumped in my lap. As if being a ghoul wasn't bad enough…as if knowing that vampires were real weren't enough. Now I had Templars, Augustines (whatever those were), and a zombie queen (nope, still no caps) dropped on my head.

Then there was this whole memory blank thing. My first suspicion was Belinda. However, I could recall every single thing that she had told me. I doubted that she could use her powers on yours truly. Was it a possibility? Sure. I didn't trust that little vamp any further than I could spit…and I don't spit; it's a nasty habit.

By the time the glow on the horizon grew into the night skyline of Portland, my teeth had gone back to normal and my fingers and toes were almost there. They come out like a switchblade, but they retract over time, and always at their own pace. I have considered starting a stopwatch, but the situation never seems to be one that my mind pipes up and shouts, "Hey, hit that timer!" So I have no idea if they retract with any sort of consistency.

"And that is all you can remember seeing?" I asked—for probably the hundredth time in the past ten minutes.

"I wouldn't have seen it at all if you hadn't staggered like you were just learning to walk on heels."

"Wait…what do you mean?" She hadn't said a word about me staggering before.

"You took a step and then your knees buckled and I thought you were going to fall. My immediate thought was that somebody had shot you with a sniper rifle."

I zoomed along down the highway in silence for a few minutes. I didn't have any idea what she was talking about. My knees buckled? The only time that I ever had any trouble controlling what my legs did was during—

"There was a smell," I whispered. A little snippet of memory broke loose. When it all came, it was like a light being flicked on in a dark room. At first there was nothing, then there was everything all at once. It took my mind a moment to clean everything up and put it where it belonged, but once I had basically reorganized my mind, it was all there…I think.

It sorta reminded me of my ten-year high school reunion. I had shown up at the ritzy little golf club that had been selected to host that first mixer where we are all supposed to see who got fat, who got bald, and compare divorces.

High school was a funny time for me. My freshman year I went into summer break barely discernable from the boys. The boob fairy had skipped my house once again. Couple that with braces which came with the oh-so-sexy headgear, and I was a crazy mother and a bad girls' locker room incident away from being about as popular as *Carrie*.

When I showed up on the first day of school my sophomore year after a summer at my cousins' place in Florida, I was tan, down to just my retainer, and was sprinting towards my eventual 38DD finish line. All of a sudden, I was being asked out, I even joined the cheerleading squad. By the time that I graduated, I was the homecoming queen and had my pick of boys for the prom.

So when I showed up at the reunion (two hours after a lunch shift at The Olive Garden) more than one person was probably snickering. I hadn't done anything or gone anyplace. I was still listening to the same music and had held on to my big hair and Spandex. I actually pulled in to the parking lot cranking *18 and Life* by Skid Row. After getting the evil glare from all the fuddy-duddies hitting yellow balls at the driving range thingy, I strutted in to the big open bar area and froze. Nobody had bothered to tell me it was semi-formal. Maybe they did in really small letters at the bottom of the invitation and I missed it. In any case, I was beyond underdressed for this little soiree.

Since I didn't have Lisa Kudrow as my wingman, I felt like an absolute idiot. There was no happy ending that night. I slipped out as soon as I could and skipped the rest of the week-end's festivities. That night, with a bottle of Southern Comfort, I started replaying a bunch of my high school memories. I dug out my yearbook and started browsing at all the entries.

"…never forget that night at the drive-in…"

"…that time in the pool…"

"…under the bleachers during the assembly…"

I had gone through three years of an illusion. I had thought that I was popular and funny. The only thing I was…was easy. And then I started remembering it all. But I was remembering it how it actually was versus this shiny, perfect thing that I had created in my mind.

Somebody…or better yet…some*thing* had messed with my mind! Well Ava Birch is nobody's fool. And now that I was aware, I would figure out what happened and make sure that it never happened again. I just hope it didn't involve wearing a tin foil hat.

***

"Ava!" Lisa called from the kitchen.

"What?" I was getting dressed and preparing for another trip to Estacada. I had given Lisa strict orders to get my attention the moment that she saw anything strange. A woman unaffected by the wind definitely fell into that category. If I was bringing her along on this little venture, then I needed her eyes peeled for stuff.

"You have a phone call!" Hmm. Now that might just fall in the "anything strange" category.

I became a ghoul after allowing my weak mind to win out in the argument that life would be better off without me involved. Who knew that suicide is the last step to ghoulishness? Anyways, I must have been dead on my bathroom floor for a few days before I came to and entered this new life. The problem I had initially was getting over the idea that my place of employment hadn't so much as called when I didn't show up for work. You can totally throw out the thing that I wasn't even that good of an employee.

Turn on the news any night and you see stories about some girl or another coming up missing. I hadn't even rated that kind of response. Here we are almost a year later and nobody from my past ever came looking for me. So a phone call? Yeah, that falls in the "strange" category for sure. Heck, the only reason I still even had a phone was…damn…I have no idea!

I went downstairs where Lisa was holding the thing like it was poisonous. Seriously, is it that strange?

"Hello?" I used my most pleasant voice. After all, I could be some sort of sweepstakes winner or something. They still have those…right?

"Am I speaking to Miss Ava Birch?" an equally pleasant-sounding voice said from the other end.

"Yes you are. And who might this be?"

"This *might* be a lot of things," the voice answered with a laugh. You know the type. It is the kind where you are absolutely sure that they are laughing *at* you and not *with* you. "However, for now you can just call me Adrianna."

"I can think of a few other things that I *could* call you." Yes, two can play at this game. I had no idea who this was, but I was certain that she was already on my last nerve. Maybe she was a friend of Belinda's.

"My name is…Adrianna Montevicci."

The way she said those five words (did you just go back and count? Sheesh!), it was like she expected them to mean something to me. Too bad for her.

"You were in Estacada last night, correct." That was a statement, not a question. Okay, big whoop-di-doo, so she knew where I was last night. Anybody could have known. It wasn't like I was keeping it a secret. "You had a young girl with you." Still no big deal. "And you stood outside the Suds Shack and had a lengthy conversation with a blonde vampire." Okay, just got interesting.

"So, Adrianna, I can call you that…right? I mean you don't sound old or nothing, so I probably don't have to call you Ms. Montevicci or ma'am, right?"

There was a brief pause. I believe I felt a slight chill come through the receiver.

"Perhaps this conversation would be better if we met in person," Adrianna said. The only thing being that I wasn't too thrilled with how she said it. Imagine if spiders suddenly had the ability to speak. Now, picture them calling up all the flies and little flying bugs in the neighborhood and inviting them over.

"Maybe I should pick the place and time?" It was the best I could think of on the fly (no pun intended). I have had a few friends who dipped into the online dating thing the past few years. Well, 'friends' is probably overstating it, but you get the picture. So the number one thing I always heard them talking about was that you always met in a very public place that first time just in case they were total creeps.

"Okay," Adrianna agreed. Did she sound amused? Hmm.

"Meet me at the Voodoo Doughnut on Davis," I said.

"How cute." The way she said those two very simple words made me want to slap her. If I didn't know better, I would swear that she was toying with me. That image of the spider kept coming to mind.

"You gonna be there or not?"

"I will, and may I suggest that you not bring your little human friend with you when you come."

Before I could say a thing, she hung up. Now I was more than just a little concerned. Not only did she know about what Belinda was, but she also referred to Lisa as 'my' human. That screamed supernatural. The problem I had was that I just did not know enough about what might be out there. I guess the only thing to do was to go and meet this spider...er, I mean, woman.

I went back up to my room and grabbed my larger carry bag. I'm sorry, girls. I just can't call that thing a purse. You could fit a small child in it.

I went into my closet and found a few necessities: silver cross, holy water, *all three* kinds of salt, a decorative wooden stake and mallet that Lisa had purchased online. It was supposed to be a novelty item...if they only knew. I had no clue if any of this stuff would be helpful, but I wasn't going to just walk in and meet whoever this was and not be at least a little prepared.

4

Sunglasses at Night

"So you are just going to meet this person with no sort of backup?" Lisa huffed.

"I made sure that we would meet in a public place," I said as I tossed my bag in the passenger seat.

"Yeah…and that worked out so well in Estacada. A vampire snuck up on you, hexed me, and vanished into thin air. And shall we bring up the whole chunk of your memory that you lost?"

"I got it back," I insisted. At least I think I did…most of it at least.

"This is a bad idea, Ava." There was something in Lisa's voice that I wasn't used to hearing. That's probably why I didn't know what it was right away. It took me a few minutes.

"Are you worried about me?"

"Of course I am, you idiot!" Lisa actually had that shiny look in her eyes, the type people get when they are right on the verge of crying.

"Look, I really appreciate it…you have no idea how much." And she didn't. Maybe that was part of the problem. Somewhere along the way, we stopped really telling people what they meant. Sort of like that joke, "Of course I love you, I told you once, didn't I? If it changes, I'll let you know."

It was another one of those moments. When I had killed myself, not even my neighbors missed me. That was mostly because they had no idea who I was. I doubt that I had said more than a dozen words to all the other residents in my apartment complex back in those days. I kept to myself and they did the same. If somebody showed up on my doorstep with a casserole when I moved in, I *probably* would have waited for them to leave before I scraped it into the trash. Hey! Who knows what they put in that thing, right?

I had simply become accustomed to having nobody ask or care about my well-being. Now that I did, I don't think that I had really been appreciating it.

"Look," I turned to face Lisa and give her my full attention, "I know that this might be a little bit dangerous. But that is also why you can't come with me. Morgan warned me against involving you in this case at all, and I did it anyways because I didn't think."

"What if something happens to you?"

"First off, the house is bought and paid for, and second you are listed as my beneficiary."

"I don't care about any of that!" Lisa snapped.

"Well if you are worried about me, don't be. I'm a ghoul for crying out loud!"

"That doesn't mean you are invincible," Lisa shot back. "Nothing is really immortal. That is the problem with things like vampires, they think they can't be hurt all the way up to the point when somebody drives a stake through their heart. You already know that you can't be out in the sun, but I bet there are other ways to hurt you that we don't know."

I wanted to *know* what brought on this sudden display of emotion. I knew it had to be more than just simple PMS. She was almost in tears...correct that. The first couple started to trickle down her cheek.

"If I promise to be careful, will that make you feel better?" I asked.

"No," Lisa said. "You won't mean to, but you will do or say something stupid and get yourself in trouble. It isn't a bad thing, it's just the way you are, Ava."

I was almost hurt. The only problem was that I knew what

she was saying. I couldn't keep my big mouth shut.

"So what will help you feel better?" I asked.

"Take me with you," Lisa insisted.

I thought it over. I could almost imagine the little angel and devil sitting on my shoulder arguing. If I took her with me, she would feel better, but I would possibly be putting her in serious danger. So is this what it was like being a parent? I mean, I feel responsible for her, but at the same time, I want her to still be my friend. One thing was for sure, when this whole thing was over, I was going out and buying some books on the whole parenting subject.

"Fine, you can go, but you have to do what I say," I conceded.

"Okay!" Lisa was already zooming around to the other side of the car and shoving my bag on the floor.

We headed for the meeting with the mysterious stranger. I tried to let my music do its magic and clear my head, but something about all of this was bothering me.

When we arrived, I found a spot to park and turned to Lisa with as serious of an expression on my face as I could muster.

"I will be going in alone. I want you to stay here in the car and keep an eye on the place. And I will be sitting close to a window. I want you to keep an eye on me."

Lisa nodded. "Just don't forget to grab me a Cock-N-Balls!"

For those of you who have not been to Voodoo Doughnut, you are missing out on quite an experience. They have some very creative people coming up with the names of their doughnuts. This one is a local favorite. I imagine that women order it more often. Most men probably wince at the idea of publically announcing that they would like a Cock-N-Balls. Big sissies.

"Fine. Now sit tight and keep the doors locked."

I walked across the parking lot. I could already see that the place was empty except for the employees. I walked in and smiled at the girl behind the counter. She smiled in that way that only those who work in the service industry can truly master.

There was one bonus to coming here of all places. It was sufficiently weird enough that I did not need to spray paint myself. Wearing my sunglasses to cover my solid black eyes would be sufficient. I glanced up at the menu and caught a whiff of something nasty. I tried not to look obvious, but when I looked up and the girl in back making doughnuts met my gaze, she flashed just the tiniest glimpse of fang. Hmm…a vampire working the late night shift at Voodoo? Interesting.

"Try the Old Dirty Bastard, it is amazing," a voice almost giggled in my ear.

Remember that whole thing about me regarding how I felt about anything that could sneak up on a ghoul and a vampire? Well if I'd had anything in my bladder, it would have been rather embarrassing. However, the sound of my nails clicking on the floor was bad enough. Fortunately, I was able to slip my hands behind my back before the girl at the counter noticed.

"How about a Voodoo Dozen, you pick," I said, trying my best not to spin around and face whoever this woman was that had managed to sneak up on me and whisper in my ear. "And also one Cock-N-Balls." I had never actually ordered one, and I guess I expected a smirk or a dirty look. The girl behind the counter simply grabbed one of their famous pink boxes and started pulling an assortment of doughnuts from the various racks.

"Now—" I spun around ready to lay into this woman, but ended up standing there with my mouth open like an idiot. She was already sitting at a table with her hands folded neatly in front of her.

Fine, I thought. She could wait. I was going to stand here until my order was filled, and then I would go over and see who and what this woman was.

I paid for my doughnuts and dropped a ten in the tip jar. Now that I had taken care of my business, it was time to meet Adrianna.

As I walked across to her table, I took the time to get a really good look at her. She had dark hair, a maple syrup brunette if I had to nail down the color, and it was done in a really cute style that I could never pull off. You know that thing where it looks long on one side, but short on the other. On me it would just look like my hairdresser goofed.

Since she was dressed in *really* short shorts, I got to see her legs. Not that I go looking at other women's legs, but hers really drew my attention. She had all the appearance of somebody who should be a natural warm olive tone. Yet, they were as ivory white as the rest of her skin, but her hair had already told me that she was not an albino. However, it was the tattoos that drew me in.

You know those comedy and tragedy masks that are on the Mötley Crüe *Theater of Pain* album? Well she had one of those on each leg just above the knee. At least I thought they were tattoos until one of them yawned. I think it was the sad face.

As for her eyes, well, that was the other giveaway that she wasn't an albino. As far as I know, albinos have red eyes or pink or something. What I am certain of is that they are not all yellow where they should be white and then a sort of swirling brown and green with flecks of gold.

Yep. She was definitely a supernatural.

I took a seat across from her and tried not to be obvious as I looked out to the parking lot and checked on my Corvette...and Lisa. Of course I was checking on Lisa! I just happened to also be able to see how pretty my car looked at the same time.

Adrianna folded her hands on the table and that was when I got my next surprise. Her hands! Okay, for you to really understand this, you have to realize that Adrianna is *very* pretty. Not in that girl-next-door-pretty. Nope, she is more I-am-so-out-of-any-boy's-league pretty. But her hands? They needed that Palmolive lady or something. Her nails looked like she trimmed them with a rusty chainsaw and they were all wrinkled and pruny like she had been in the pool for a week. Basically they were gross.

"If you are worried about your little human, don't be," Adrianna said with a dismissive wave of her hand. "I agreed to meet you, so I am bound by certain rules."

"What sort of rules?" Might as well take this opportunity to learn a few things.

"Since I called for this meeting, I cannot make any attack on you or your representatives."

"Umm, I guess that is nice," I said with a shrug. "So-o who set these rules?"

"Are you going to waste all of our time on such trivial matters?"

That was the first time I noticed something odd about her voice. There was a barely noticeable sort of echo. No…it wasn't *exactly* an echo. You know when cheap horror films have that sort of layered voice thing that they use when somebody is possessed? It was like Bowser from Sha Na Na was repeating everything that Adrianna said, but just a fraction of a second late and from the same mouth.

"Look," I decided that I was going to be assertive. Maybe I had been too much of a pushover when I first met Morgan. Now she thought that she could just walk all over me. "I have no idea who…or *what* for that matter…you are, but since you called me and supposedly can't hurt me right now, I have some questions."

"Fine." Adrianna sat back. I guess I had the floor…or the table.

"Do I get a certain number of questions?" That might be good to know in advance. "And this one doesn't count if I do!" *Whew! Didn't want to get caught with that little trick.*

"How about we be fair?" Adrianna proposed. "You ask a question and then I ask one. We trade off five each. Then we can get down to business if there is anything that remains to be discussed once we have finished."

It sounded fair, but I bet anybody who has signed a deal with The Devil thought it was a good deal at first. Hey, did you know that you could actually do that? I was blown away. You are probably wondering how I know this. Yeah, well one of the ghosts that I have talked to in the past made one. I guess she asked to live forever. Somehow, The Devil managed to find a loophole in his contract that allowed her existence as a ghost to count as living by equating living with existing or something along those lines. I tend to space out a bit when she starts talking and so I may have missed some of the details.

"…and nobody has to die tonight."

Wait...what? I hate it when my mind wanders. I mean it has its advantages because it makes it easier to go to my 'happy' place—damn, I'm doing it again, aren't I?

"So who goes first?" No sense in making her angry by showing that I was not paying her the slightest bit of attention. Besides, the important thing I heard was that nobody 'has to die tonight.'

"Since I invited you to meet, I will *allow* you to go first," Adrianna said. That deep voice thing was gone. I wonder if that meant she only did it at certain times. Although there was the way she said the word 'allow' like she meant it in the most literal sense.

"Okay." I wanted to make sure I didn't ask anything stupid. After just a moment of thought, I had it! The first question was so obvious. How could I ask anything else?

"You are obviously not human, so just what exactly are you?" It would help to know just what I was dealing with.

"Silly girl, I thought you already knew that one. I am The Queen of the Zombies."

5

Always Something There to Remind Me

If I would have been eating or drinking anything, I would have done an excellent spit-take. As it was, my wide-open mouth was probably sufficient.

"Ah." Adrianna smiled and clicked her horrendous fingernails on the surface of the table. "You either know who I am, or have heard tales."

I tried to reconcile the person I had just been told was responsible for wiping out like half the population of the world with this petite—and let's face it, if not for the hands, she would be sickeningly hot, not that men notice things like hands when confronted with curves that scream Victoria's Secret—brunette that sat here smiling like nothing was wrong. It just did not seem to add up. And then there was the name: Adrianna. Not very European in my opinion. Wasn't that the girl from *Rocky*? Now had she said Monique or Giselle, I could have seen the connection a little clearer.

"So, since knowledge is power, my question to you is this…who told you about me?"

Well, it wasn't like I owed Belinda anything. "A vampire named Belinda."

Adrianna mulled this over and seemed okay with the an-

43

swer. But now I was suffering from stage fright. Yes, I had The Queen of the Zombies (yep…she gets the caps now) sitting right here, and I had four questions left to ask. The only problem was that now I didn't know which ones. After all, if she had wiped out half the world, then what was she doing in Estacada, Oregon? And was she really setting zombies loose out there in the woods? Should I think local or global?

"Are you letting zombies loose in the woods of Estacada?" That seemed like a pretty important question.

"I…" Adrianna started, but her voice seemed to fade and got a little strangled. She shot me a dirty look like I had just done something wrong. "The zombies in the woods outside of Estacada are mine, yes."

She took a deep breath and seemed really annoyed for some reason. Since I hadn't done anything wrong—that I knew of—I decided to let it go.

"And just what sort of creature might you be?" Adrianna leaned forward. I wondered if that is how a mouse feels when the cat has it by the tail.

"I'm a ghoul," I said. That seemed like an easy one. I was a bit perplexed that she had to ask considering how old she must be if she had started the Black Plague.

"How interesting."

Adrianna had a new expression on her face. I remembered back to when I was just a little girl and my mom took me and Sophia Riggs to see the movie *The Jungle Book* for my ninth birthday. This was that Disney cartoon version with those talking vultures that were sort of beatnik knockoffs of The Beatles. (Of course I didn't get that reference until I was much older.) In the cartoon, I remember being so afraid of that damn tiger that anytime I heard somebody speak with a British accent for the next two years, I would run and cry. There was something sinister in that tiger's smile…kudos to the cartoonists on that one. My point being, I was seeing something in Adrianna's eyes now that had not been there a moment ago. It was like she was staring at a buffet after having been without food for at least a month.

"Are you planning on trying to wipe out the world again?"

Yay for me. I was thinking of everybody else like a good little girl.

"No, and how are you doing that?" Adrianna snapped after getting that look on her face like I was kicking her or pinching her under the table; which I wasn't if you are thinking that.

"Doing what?" At least those are the words that came to the very tip of my tongue. However, something seemed to click in my brain and all I could do was answer the question. "I have no idea what you are talking about."

"Okay, stop talking!" Adrianna was using that creepy voice trick again, but the low voice was actually a bit louder than her regular voice. If my guess was correct and that was tied to her being angry, then she was starting to get really pissed.

"But—" I was about to ask what was wrong when she put one of those super gross hands on my mouth. That certainly shut me up. It smelled like candy.

"We are bound by our agreement to ask and answer five questions." She said all of that like it was really important. "I initially thought that you were being exceptionally clever when you chose to meet here of all places. This location and the other have certain aspects that can be either a help or a hindrance for the supernaturals who might frequent the establishment."

Now I had a bunch of questions. The problem was, every single time that I opened my mouth, Adrianna made for me with one of those hands. If she kept doing that, I was going to end up having a snack. And trust me, it wouldn't be one of the dough-nuts.

However, I can't begin to explain how absolutely repulsed by them I was on the visual side of things. But perhaps this would help clarify. I would rather lick Belinda's nether parts. Considering the fact that I have never even been the teensiest bit bi-curious and couple it with that whole thing about her mere presence bringing to me the smell of hot garbage frosted with the goo from the bottom of a Dumpster and perhaps you are on the same page with me.

"I request that we suspend our agreement in regards to our questions. If you agree, then you must state, 'I agree to suspend our contract' and then prick your finger and let a drop of your blood and mine mingle."

This all seemed a bit too weird, but she was unequivocally serious. I nodded in agreement and dug through my carry bag for something that I could use to cut my finger. I had plenty of heavy artillery in the way of stakes and mallets, but I had to dig until I found a sharpener for my eyeliner. That would have to do.

After slicing my finger, I must admit that I was shocked when some dark goopy stuff came out. I guess it was blood; Adrianna didn't seem to have any problems with it. I waited as she cut her finger. It was a serious disappointment. Blood. Just regular old red blood. I imagine that if it were tested or something it would probably be interesting to some degree, but on the table, all I saw was a drop of just-plain-blood.

It was only a little strange when she started mumbling a bunch of stuff in a funny language. Having worked as a waitress, I am familiar enough with Spanish to know it wasn't *español*. Beyond that, I didn't have a clue.

Finally, she made it extra nasty by spitting on the blood finger-painting that she had created. I looked around. Of course the employees were completely ignoring us—even the vampire. I waited for the lights to flicker or for a sudden breeze to kick up.

Nothing.

I looked up at Adrianna with an expression that I hoped read "Is that it? Can I talk now?" She made a clicking sound with her tongue and grabbed her purse.

"Seriously?" I blurted when she pulled out a little compact and did some touch up work on her make-up.

"What?" Adrianna snorted. "So this isn't that 'animal safe' crap. Look, if it takes a few monkeys or rabbits to make sure that this stuff doesn't run, who cares?" She pulled out a tube and ran the little wand over her lips. I had to admit, it was an awesome shape of purple. I tried to sneak a look at the label, but she stuffed it into her purse.

"I take it we can ask questions now." I was super careful with how my voice sounded so that it didn't come out as a question just in case.

"We have approximately ten minutes," Adrianna said before taking a sip from her cup of coffee.

"So what the hell just happened?" I had to ask.

"You really are clueless, aren't you?" Adrianna laughed. It is one of those kinds of laughs you would expect to hear from Martha Stewart if you told her a fart joke.

"If you are just going to sit there and offend me—" I started to get up. I didn't need to sit here and be abused. There were plenty of people that would come to my house and do it. Hey, at least I would be able to sit on my comfy couch instead of sitting on this hard plastic.

"Actually, that was not meant as an offense. I am just truly surprised that you did not know what you were doing."

"So what did I do?"

"Well, this place sits on a natural *ju-ju*." When I just stared at her with my best blank expression, she continued. "A *ju-ju* is like a charm. It can be good or bad, but it has power. This one took our agreement and bound us to it since we are both supernatural. It would not allow us to be deceptive in our responses, and it would not allow us to ask a question until we answered the one posed by the other."

That explained why I had felt so compelled to answer and had not been able to ask the question that had come to mind. But there was also that little bit about not being able to be deceptive. I wonder if that had anything to do with the nasty looks she had shot me just before answering a couple of my questions. That would be good information to keep in mind.

"So what you did to stop it or pause or whatever, that was magic?"

Adrianna laughed. Once again it was the kind of laugh that made me want to reach across the table and slap her. She was looking at me and treating me in a way that made Morgan's treatment of me seem almost kind. The biggest problem was not what she was saying, it was all in the looks and the tone.

You ever know somebody like that? If you shared what they said to piss you off, your boyfriend or whatever would look at you and say something stupid like, "So what's the problem?"

The problem is that when you were at Jamie Cowan's slumber party and they were all talking about their favorite songs, and you heard them mention *Love Song*, how were you supposed to know that they were talking about Broadway musicals and something called *Pippin*, and not the band Tesla? Stupid Jenny Atkinson. I was doing it again, I could tell by the look on Adrianna's face that I had just missed something.

"Excuse me," I apologized. Well, technically that isn't really an apology, but she should know what I meant.

"Is this a cultural thing?" Adrianna huffed.

"What?"

"You Americans are an incredibly self-absorbed bunch, aren't you?"

Okay, I'm not what you would consider patriotic. Sure, I cried when all the memorials and stuff happened after 9/11. And I stand for the National Anthem or whatever that song is that nobody has been able to sing properly since Whitney Houston did it at that football game during one of those wars over in one of those deserty places. But it is like when somebody picks on a member of your family, you may not like him or her, but the only person allowed to pick on them is you!

"*Us* Americans?" I exclaimed. "And what country are you from? Wait!" I raised my hand and cut her off before she could answer. "Nobody cares. You know why? Because this country totally rocks!" So it wasn't the most inspirational speech. It wasn't going to win any awards or make a great scene if I ever became the inspiration for a movie or television series like that bitch Sookie.

"Yes, well, be that as it may..." Adrianna began.

You have to be seeing the same thing that I am here. She is a total bitch, right? I mean, who says that? *Be that as it blah-bady-blah-blah.*

"...I was trying to explain that all I managed to do is postpone the binding. We will be forced to resume it in just a few minutes, so perhaps you should clear your head...not that there should be any problems with that."

See? She didn't need to say that. She just had to get a little dig on me.

"So how is it that you came to Estacada looking for me? Because I initially thought one thing, but now I can see I was mistaken."

Okay, I had no idea what point she was trying to make, but I knew she was implying that I am an idiot. However, one thing was certain; she didn't know anything about Morgan. That *had* to be important.

Now, say what she would— Damn! Now I was thinking like her. I don't think I'm the kind of gal that would say "say what she would" any more than I would say "Be that as it may."

Great, now I am spacing out on myself!

So the point that I was trying to make is that her not knowing about Morgan seemed to be important. Since we were going to be bound to answer questions again in a minute, something like that could wait. Let her pay for it.

"You want to know something like that...ask in about ten minutes or whenever this little parlay is over."

"Parlay? Where on earth would you pick up a word like that?"

"I've seen the *Pirates of the Caribbean* movies." Take that Little-Miss-Smarty-Pants!

"Yes, well, be that as it may (See!), perhaps I have underestimated you. I can assure you that I will not be doing so from here on out."

Hmm, I wondered if that was a good thing or not. The best thing about having people think that I am a bit ditzy is that they have little to no expectations. Having this self-proclaimed Queen of the Zombies thinking that I am a threat might come back to bite me in the ass.

"...so when we resume this little mutual interrogation, you are now aware of the rules."

Damn! I was really going to have to stop that. I seem to always space out when people say something important.

"Fine." I tried my best to make that sound confident. I think Adrianna's lips curved up in a very slight smile. So she was back to being the spider.

"We each have two questions remaining," Adrianna said. "Once we have finished, we will both be free to go our separate ways. However, I want to extend an offer to you right now."

"I'm listening." *Focus, Ava.*

"Come with me."

That was not at all what I expected. What on earth could she want or need *me* for. And I was pretty sure that Belinda had at least implied that she was evil.

"Why?" That seemed like a simple question.

"Like you, I believe that I will save an answer like that for when it counts for something."

I began to feel a tingle in my head. It was like this one time when I was really little, like six or seven. We went to visit some relative who was dying and all the kids were told to stay outside while the grownups talked. I came to this fence, and above the barbed wire was this single strand of silvery wire. One of my cousins told me that it would bite me if I touched it. For the rest of the day, I stayed away from the fence, but my mind had to know how a fence could "bite" me. I guess you already figured out how it went from there, so I don't need to share. Anyways, the rest of the day I had this tingle in my hands. Right now, I had a very similar feeling in my head.

"…and perhaps we could ask your little human friend."

I told myself I was going to listen. And she mentioned Lisa; that meant it was something really important.

"What?" When Adrianna smiled, I knew that she had just used my tendency to daydream against me.

"I said that if my plan is to work, I need to find a virgin and perhaps we can talk with your little human friend." There was that smug look that I was really starting to hate. "Now, how is it that you came to Estacada looking for me?"

This was my chance to play it cool. I had seen plenty of movies where the evil villain would ask the hero a question and the hero would answer it in such a way that it wasn't really a lie, but it didn't provide much help or insight. Unfortunately, I didn't have any fancy-shmancy screen writers feeding me dialog. I was on my own here.

50

I glanced outside and noticed my Corvette. I had it! My 'ah-ha' moment bloomed in my head like those videos that are sped up and show flowers opening almost instantly. I was all set to answer the question. The words 'In my car' were on the tip of my tongue when I felt a jolt of pain to my head.

"Somebody was about to be deceptive," Adrianna said with a snotty little laugh.

At least now I knew why she had been giving me those dirty looks earlier. She had been trying the exact same thing. Maybe she wasn't going to lie, but she was certainly not going to say the whole truth. I formed the answer in my head and waited for another brain jolt. Nothing.

"I was looking into a report that zombies had been spotted in the area." I waited another second for any pain, but nothing happened. *Ha, take that!*

"I see." That was all she said, but I didn't like it. Had I been that obvious? I was pretty sure that I only thought that 'Ha, take that!' remark.

Oh well, now it was my turn and I only had this one last question that I could be guaranteed any sort of truthful answer. I was already very aware that this Queen of the Zombies would lie to me the first chance she got. And that is when it came to me. I had a question that I could ask her that she couldn't just weasel out of. The only problem was that I wasn't sure if it would do me any good. Oh well, here goes nothing.

"How did you become the Queen of the Zombies?"

Bingo! Not only did I get to see this prissy piece of Euro-trash actually do a spit-take with her coffee, but the look on her face was something that I might cherish forever. I already shared how I was basically a pirate's dream in my freshman year with my sunken chest. Well it was that first day back to school of my sophomore year that gave me one of the first such moments in my life.

From the time I was in about fourth grade, one boy in particular had made it a point to try and make my life a living hell: Mike Meyers (no relation to that monster from the *Halloween* movies, but there wasn't that much difference in my opinion). It graduated over the years from tugging on my ponytail to noogies. But in my freshman year, he cornered me with his little pack of goons. I didn't know what he had in mind, but I was braced for the worst. He leaned in, and with that day's lunch of fish sticks on his breath and in his teeth, he said for all to hear, "I was gonna give you a titty twister, but I don't have all day to find 'em!"

I don't think the flames on my face went out for a week. For the rest of the year, I heard things like "Ain't that false advertising when you wear a bra, Ava?" When I came back the next year...guess who was standing in the doorway as I walked in to school?

Focus, Ava! Now is not the time to be letting your mind wander. I folded my hands on the table in front of me and flashed my best smile at Adrianna, who was wincing. Guess she was trying to lie.

6

Like A Virgin

"I was born in a village just outside of Naples, Italy," she finally began after a very long pause and a few more winces. In fact, she paused for so long that I was momentarily afraid that I had spaced out again and she had already answered. "I was named Adrianna D' Assandrio and the daughter of a whore…"

Geez, I hated my mom when I was growing up, too, but that's kind of harsh.

"When I was sixteen, I was wed to the son of our village elder. He died two weeks later and I was blamed. His grandmother came down from Rome just before the funeral. She went into the tomb, and when she came out, she claimed that I had murdered my husband.

"A day later, I was thrown in to jail and sentenced to death. I was to be burned at the stake for my crime at sunset. All those stories about witch trials that happened in this country are almost funny. Had any of those accused actually been witches, they would have never been killed quite so easily. I was not about to be executed by these simple fools."

Adrianna took another long pause. I could tell that she was having a rough time telling me this stuff. I imagine that she was not the sort to share a bunch of her personal life with others. I began to wonder if she had ever told this to anybody.

"I had to cast a summoning if I was going to escape this.

The problem with that is the fact that demons don't care much for the daylight. It tends to make them weak…"

I was really glad that there was some sort of force—*ju-ju* or whatever you call it—compelling Adrianna to tell the truth, because this was starting to seem like a load of horse puckey. And the way she mentioned summoning demons, like it was no big deal, was loading my brain up with some questions for Morgan. In fact, the next time I saw her, she had some serious 'splainin' to do.

"…when the deal was made, I must have been careless with my words. A demon is always looking for an angle to give you what you ask for without giving you what you want. I made a mistake somewhere."

I sat there for a few moments, waiting to see what else she would say, but she didn't say a word. She was done. I know that I had drifted a couple of times, but nothing serious. I considered all that she had told me. I didn't see where there was anything in the narrative that was going to help. Maybe I should have asked something else.

"So," Adrianna said with her Cheshire grin as she flipped that one long lock of hair that hung down in her face, "now I guess it is my turn to ask my last question."

Once again, Adrianna was silent. I imagine that she was trying to find that perfect question. She wanted to make sure that she asked something that gave her some relevant information. The only problem with that was the fact that I wasn't all that relevant.

"What would it take for you to join me?"

That question hung in the air, and I bet the look on my face was priceless. I hated the fact that this was the end of our session. And hadn't she implied earlier that she wanted me to join her? I think so, but that was one of those Ava moments where I had let my mind wander way down the path. Still, it never even came to me in the slightest to ask her why she would want me to join her.

I gave the question some thought. Actually, I gave my answer some thought. It was almost like playing a game of hide-

and-seek with this *ju-ju* induced pain. I was not anxious to experience that feeling again. That was probably one of the biggest reasons I was so careful not to have children. I'd been to the hospital with a friend of mine once who was going in to labor. She was one of those workout types. If I had a dollar for all the times I'd heard her say, 'No pain, no gain!' I could have given up waitressing.

She had her baby in her actual room. I don't know anything about having babies. I guess I expected them to rush her off to the delivery room. This place didn't have one except for when there was a problem. I guess the thing was for the woman to have the baby in her actual room; something about making it a more 'complete and relaxing experience' for the mother and baby. Personally, I don't think a baby cares where it is born.

I made the mistake of staying in her room because I just assumed that sooner or later they would take her out. There was this one moment where she let loose with this scream. It started as a low moan that grew to a growl that changed to an oh-my-God-this-thing-is-ripping-me-open shriek. I doubt anybody even noticed me leave. She never did call me again.

So I let my mind ease towards what I thought might be an answer, but was a little shaky about just how little I was going to say. When I let the answer fully form, I waited for a second. Then it was my turn to smile big and let her feel a bit concerned.

I watched her eyes. I wanted to see her reaction. I wanted to put it in a bottle and spray it on my pillow.

"Nothing."

It was even better than I had hoped. You know that thing they do in cartoons where somebody gets hit in the mouth and all their teeth fracture and then shatter and crash down leaving nothing but a gaping hole? Well if her face was made of glass, it would have been all over the floor.

There was just one problem. I was expecting her to say something snotty and that would be that. What I got was a look that I am pretty sure could have done damage to a regular human. In fact, I am certain that when she shot that look at me, she expected me to burst into flames or something.

"Fine," she said.

Crap, there was that deep voice lurking under her regular one again. Yep, she was mad.

"If that is the way you want things, know that I will not be extending this offer to you again. Once we leave here, I will consider you a threat."

"So what does that mean?" I asked.

"No more questions, Ava. You are on your own from here on out."

"Well then…maybe I will give you a little bit of a warning," I blurted. For the life of me I have no idea what possessed me to open my mouth, but here we were, and I had her full attention. "I will give you twenty-four hours to leave. I don't care what you do someplace else, but you aren't starting some silly zombie apocalypse here in my neck of the woods."

"That is cute," Adrianna said. She didn't smile anymore, and for some reason, that really bothered me. "But perhaps it is time to give you a little warning. I am The Queen of the Zombies. I was made immortal by a demon and have existed for hundreds of years. You are…nothing. We are no longer bound to one another, and once you leave these premises…"

She let that hang in the air. It was not a threat. She was telling me that my ass was in serious trouble. I was considering just how the employees here a Voodoo Doughnut would feel about me moving in.

"Oh, you think that I care about you?" Adrianna laughed. And now I wished she wasn't doing that. "You serve me no purpose whatsoever…but your little friend…she is just a child, true?"

"You touch her and I will rip you apart," I hissed. And as if to support that threat, my fingers and toes went switchblade. To add a bit of impact, good old sharkmouth decided to show up.

"My, my!" Adrianna had the sense to look worried. "That is something new. I am almost sorry we don't have a few more questions."

"Mrrglph," I said. Dammit! That was probably the wittiest comeback I'd managed to think of in my life, and it was wasted

56

on my sharkmouth. And wouldn't you just love to know what I was going to say.

"Trust me when I say that she won't feel a thing," Adrianna said as she stood. I was immediately struck by how cruel life was when somebody that is obviously so evil has curves like this lady. It just isn't fair!

I started to get up, and then I guess I saw Adrianna for the first time as she really exists. Her perfect skin was mottled and gray, her stylish hair hung in greasy clumps. Those eyes that were so shiny and a deep chocolate-brown flecked with green and gold were milky and oozing dark liquid that ran like tears down her face. Funny thing, now her hands which had been her worst feature were actually her least icky. There was one other unfortunate aspect to the change.

My knees buckled, and the closest thing that I can compare it to for a human is to suddenly be dunked in a vat of Godiva fudge. I heard a wet splat and was embarrassed when I looked down to see a long line of drool hanging from my lower lip.

"Out!" a voice barked.

Both Adrianna and I looked up to see the vampire that I'd noticed working back in the doughnut kitchen standing in front of the counter. She had obviously put the whammy on the girl behind the counter, because she was standing with a blank look that I'd seen on Lisa's face more than once when Belinda had been near.

"Get in your kitchen, little girl," Adrianna said with almost none of her regular voice. It was almost fully the deep, bass sounding one now, and it had a dry echo that you felt in your teeth. Well…at least I did.

The vampire paused as if she was unsure. Then, like all vampires do (although I've only met a couple, so perhaps I am being unfair), this one obviously felt it was dealing with an inferior being. She let her fangs show and her eyes went a really pretty shade of ruby red. I guess she was still seeing the glamour version of Adrianna. Perhaps she wasn't paying attention to the dark swirly stuff that was flowing off her like steam. Whatever it was, the vampire just did not think it through.

It launched across the room in one of those movie-style blurs. I only had enough time to appreciate that Hollywood had done a good job of capturing that aspect before the two were face-to-face. The vampire opened its mouth and plunged into Adrianna's throat. I was super jealous. In this state, she smelled so yummy that I was already deciding the best way to deal with the whole 'Queen of the Zombies' problem: have her for breakfast. (See what I did there?)

I guess vampires don't have the same taste palate as we ghouls. She flew back and began spitting and hacking like a cat with a monster hairball. Seriously, at one point, she was scrubbing at her tongue with her hands.

"*What* are you?" the vampire managed after hawking up a big tar-like glob that hit the floor and actually dissolved through the tiles in a steaming, bubbling flash that left a lingering smell better than any bakery.

"Silly little vampire," Adrianna cooed. Yeah, cooed. Hey, you weren't there, but that is what she did. "I am The Queen of the Zombies."

And seriously, when she says it, you can actually hear the capitalization of each word. Yeah, even the word the; it's crazy. Somebody has a pretty high opinion of herself...besides me that is.

The vampire seemed confused. It appeared pretty obvious that she didn't know a zombie queen from a drag queen at this point. And typical of a vampire, she considered herself at the top of the food chain.

"Well I don't care what delusions you live under, this location has rules. If you are part of this community, then you are bound to them just like any other ghost, ghoul (she glanced at me, yay!), or goblin. The magic here is older than time and binds us all to its rule. This is a place of peace. Wars have ended at these tables and you will not violate the sanctity of the *ju-ju*..."

I had to stifle a giggle. I'm sorry, but just say those last few words out loud, 'you will not violate the sanctity of the *ju-ju*.' Come on, it's a little funny. Like aardvark, I can't say that word without at least smiling. Tell me I'm not alone here. Somebody at least nod. Fine! But I bet you didn't say it out loud or you'd totally be on my side.

"…and do not return!" the vampire said with way more authority than you would have expected from a girl that looked like she had slipped and fallen on a piercing gun face first.

I shrugged and headed for the door. Adrianna seemed to want to test the water a bit more and stayed rooted in place for a moment; and then I saw her wince. Hmm. Maybe that *ju-ju* thing had seen about enough of The Queen of the Zombies for the time being.

I was almost to my car when I heard my name being called. She was back to a mix of regular voice and that oom-papa-mow-mow guy from the Oak Ridge Boys' song…*Elvira* I think was the title. I considered just ignoring her. Something told me I should get in my car and go home. After all, hadn't she threatened Lisa? It was starting to get fuzzy. Damn! This was what she had done last time. She had some sort of ability that allowed her to erase my memory. Actually, it didn't get erased. It was more like the keys to your car. You know you set them somewhere, you just can't, for the life of you, remember where.

"Ava," the voice said in a really demanding tone.

"What?" I spun around and tried to focus. Everything was getting kind of hazy. Hey…when did sharkmouth go away?

"I told you that our truce was over." She folded her arms under her breasts, pushing them up farther than her push-up bra already… I looked closer. The fairness fairy was a bitch! She wasn't wearing a bra! How can breasts defy gravity like that? I was hating her more every single minute. I mean seriously, she's like several hundred years old. Mine stopped looking that good about ten years ago.

"So, I will be taking your young friend with me." That snapped me out of my little trance.

"Like hell you will!" Thankfully, my fingers and toes were still sporting serious nailage.

Adrianna took a step my direction and staggered. I heard her say something, and I am pretty sure it was a string of naughty words, but it wasn't in English, so I could only guess.

"It seems that this little *ju-ju* has some lingering effects," she finally said through clenched teeth.

"And so you want to take my friend Lisa out of what...spite?" I said as I moved in between my car and The Queen of the Zombies. There was just no way that I would be letting her take Lisa.

"I can't get my zombies to stay together." Adrianna actually pouted! I mean, this was something to think about. Here was this so-called Queen of the Zombies, and she'd already done the whole 'Let's bash America' thing that so many people enjoy these days. Now she was actually pouting like Paris Hylton after being told that she would have to buy her new wardrobe at K-Mart. Don't get me wrong. I can pout with the best of them, but it was nice to see that this might simply be something inherent in our gender.

"You want to run that by me again?" I asked. Now I knew that she was under no compulsion to answer, and if she did, she could very well be lying through her teeth. Still, something about this seemed important.

"My zombies," Adrianna repeated, "they only last about an hour, and then they start to just come apart. Arms fall off, and pretty soon they are nothing but a pile of cold goo."

That sounded really gross. But it also sounded like information that I needed to know. And if I could just remember it once this little meeting was over, I'd probably be able to talk to Morgan and discover a way to stop Adrianna from whatever diabolical scheme was floating around in her brain.

"Okay," I shook my head to clear the inner monolog, "but what does that have to do with Lisa?"

"Most magic of any serious power is demon related, duh!"

Oh no she didn't! She did not just 'duh' me.

"To activate the magic...?" She left that question hanging in the air and gave me this raised eyebrow thing that Mr. Spock would have been envious of...if he were real...and standing here.

"You really don't know anything, do you?" Adrianna asked...again.

"What am I supposed to know?" I exploded. I'd had enough of all of this. I was sick of Morgan and her snide little comments. I was sick of Belinda. (No need to go any further, I was just sick of her.) I was sick of all this supernatural crap that I didn't know, but for some reason, everybody that I met from the ghosts to other vampires, and now this damn Queen of the Zombies, they all expected that I had some basic knowledge. Well enough was enough.

"I need a virgin for this to work…the blood of a virgin is the only payment that any demon strong enough to help me will accept."

She said that like it was nothing. *'Honey, while you're at the store, could you pick up eggs, milk, bread…and, oh yeah, some virgin's blood.'* Then it hit me and I started laughing. Adrianna's pout changed to a look of annoyance. I am pretty sure that she is simply not used to be dealt with in this manner.

"What is so amusing?" she asked.

"Unless there is something about Lisa that I don't know, you are out of luck there. That birth canal has already seen one passenger through it that I'm aware of…and while I'm pretty sure that was the only one, it still negates that whole 'virgin' thing you think you have here."

"But she is just a child, she can't be any more than sixteen!" Adrianna had the decency to sound shocked.

"I don't know what rock you've been hiding under, sister," and that was true, I had no clue what those Templars or Augustines had done or used to keep Adrianna locked away, "but you might have some trouble tracking down a virgin in these parts unless you are gonna snatch an infant or grade schooler."

"Unless she has experienced her twenty-third—" Adrianna began, but I couldn't help myself.

"A virgin who has had over twenty periods? Yeah, they're out there, but you can't just assume because she is young that she hasn't experimented." I paused, and then decided I just had to know. "And when you say virgin…are you talking about no sex in the textbook sense, or are you talking Clinton-defined sex.

Like if she just did some oral...or there has been this whole jump in girl's going the anal sex route. Not an alternative that I would be down with...but I have heard—"

"You must be joking!" Adrianna snapped.

"About which part? The thing about a girl who has been menstruating for over two years that is still a virgin being harder to find than a Republican working in a soup kitchen when it isn't an election year, or about the rise in oral and anal sex in—"

"Enough!" Adrianna stomped her foot.

I'd had about enough of her attitude. I was tired and depressed. I hadn't had sex with a partner in way too long and all this talk about the promiscuity of the younger generation coupled with just being tired of all the crap, and I was ready to leave.

"Listen, you can play your little games, or whatever it is that you are doing. I am going home. And I might just forget that I ever met you. And I might also tell Lisa not to remind me. But the bottom line is that I am sick of all of you. You think you're all so smart. Well you don't know much about people, none of you. You have been separated from it for so long that you have just let that little nugget of knowledge wither in your brain and die that tells you the human race might be screwed up in a lot of ways, but when its collective back is up against the wall, it fights back and comes together in a way that you will never be able to defend against."

I didn't care what she had to say after that. I got in the car, slammed the door, turned the key, and peeled out in a way that only a Corvette can.

7

Is There Something I Should Know

"So you just left?" Morgan almost sounded angry. Well good! It was about time somebody else got their panties in a bunch for a change.

"Did you miss the part about her doing the whole memory wipe thing?" I said with as much calm as I could muster. I was performing an experiment. So far, every time that I'd met up with Morgan, I'd ended up flying off the handle at some point. I was doing my best to channel my inner-Spock.

"I heard you the first three times, yes." Morgan glanced at Lisa. "And if you insist on putting your human in danger despite all my warnings, then perhaps we need to discuss having Belinda send one of her Kiss over."

"What?" Lisa and I said in unison.

"I specifically recall telling you that it might be best if you left the human home for this particular job," Morgan reminded.

"Yes, well she didn't feel like staying home," I replied after taking a moment to recover my composure after that last little remark.

"This is not something that I say lightly, Ava." Morgan actually sat on my couch and crossed her legs all proper. She had never once sat on my living room furniture at the apartment. In fact she used to make it a point to touch as little as possible. For her to actually sit down was serious stuff. "I understand your attachment to this...human. I had a human companion once. It did not end well."

I was stunned. First, at the simple fact that Morgan had once kept company with a human...that was big news. And for her to say what she had was the equivalent of pouring out her heart. This was something probably much bigger than even I was giving credit.

"So you are saying that I should let Lisa become a vampire?" That is one of those sentences that you never really imagine yourself putting to words.

"Either that, or Belinda can do something very similar to what The Queen of the Zombies (wow...I heard the capital letters in Morgan's voice, this gal must be pretty major stuff) has done to you...more than once." Morgan glanced at the teenage girl like she was making some sort of an appraisal. "She can erase her mind."

I considered some of what had happened in the past several months. On more than one occasion, Lisa's life had been in serious jeopardy.

"When you say erase—" I started, but Morgan cut me off.

"Unfortunately she cannot do something as seemingly selective as this Adrianna creature, but we can put some of our people in place to assist her with getting her life in order."

"Excuse me!" Lisa jumped out of her chair like it had been hit with a jolt of electricity. "I am sitting right here. Perhaps before you two start deciding my fate, somebody may want to ask me what the hell I think about all of this being turned into a vampire crap or having my brain deleted."

"Lisa—" I raised my hands, holding them out in front of me. Why do we do that? I mean, do we seriously believe that if we simply hold our hands up, the person we are trying to calm down will just say, 'Oh, okay' and relax?

"No, Ava!" she snapped. "I will have a say in this. If there is something you want to tell me about a certain mission and what the dangers may be, then fine. But I can make my own decisions.

64

I'm not stupid."

"I never said you were," I countered. "But you have to realize that some of the stuff that has happened is far more dangerous for you than for me. I would feel terrible if something happened to you."

"And I can decide for myself if it is a danger that I am willing to take. After all, I came with you *after* you ate my boyfriend, didn't I?"

She had a good point. However, I would perhaps remind her later that I hadn't eaten her *boy*friend. He was a grown man…a pedophile when you got right down to it since he was almost forty and she was still just sixteen…fifteen at the time he knocked her up. But this wasn't about her choice in men; I could save that speech for later.

"Actually," Morgan's voice cut through the room almost like it was magic. I even felt the temperature drop just a little, "you have very little idea what you are doing."

Lisa began to protest, but Morgan shot her a look that reminded me of that scene in Carrie when people were trying to escape the gym during her little pig blood-induced tantrum. Her head whips around and there is this look in her eyes that lets you know that she is experiencing some serious emotion.

"You have run off with Ava on more than one occasion now when you should have remained at home. This is just the most recent example. When Belinda came to me and told me what we might be dealing with, I actually rushed over to Ava's. Unfortunately, I was too late. When I discovered that you had gone with her, I honestly never expected to see you again. Not alive at least."

"Wait," now it was my turn to be pissed, "you knew something and didn't think that maybe a phone call or text or whatever mental mumbo jumbo you can do might be a good idea to say 'Hey, Ava…Morgan here. Before you go off to Estacada, I have some information about your task that might, I don't know, save your life!'?"

"Let's not change the subject just yet, Miss Birch." Morgan turned her attention to me.

Note to self: don't get snotty with Morgan. She gets pissed in a hurry and it is very unsettling.

"When we met, I had no idea that Italian nightmare had managed to slip her bonds. She was supposedly put away so securely that the resurfacing of Atlantis would be more likely to occur."

"Huh?" Did she just say something about Atlantis? Wasn't that some sort of resort in the Caribbean? Wait! Was she talking about the *real* Atlantis? This whole supernatural thing was coming with a steep learning curve.

"Look who's talking about changing the subject," Lisa huffed.

I think both Morgan and I almost broke our necks when our heads snapped around to her. I had no idea where she was going, but the look of defiance in her face had me curious. Plus, now Morgan wasn't giving me the evil eye anymore.

"Every single time we meet and things start to get out of hand, you throw out some new monster or whatever to distract Ava. You know she will chase after it like something shiny…"

Hey! Whose side is she on? Am I that easy to distract? Wait…they're still talking. Damn! I am that easy to distract.

"…don't know what the rules are because you only give them to us when it suits you."

Morgan wasn't actually showing what a normal person would consider an open display of shock, but the fact that her mouth was open just a bit and her eyebrows had raised a fraction, well that was quite a display. She must have realized that I was staring, because her lips pressed back together and her face smoothed back to that perfect and flawless look. Seriously, if you saw her on the streets, you would swear that she'd been given a quadruple dose of Botox. Her face just always seemed frozen in that same disinterested expression.

"Fair enough," Morgan said after a moment of silence.

"What!" Lisa and I are not nearly as good at hiding our emotions.

"I guess I must reconcile myself to the fact that I have a ghoul in my district. And I suppose I will make allowances for you, Lisa."

Now I was really flabbergasted. To my knowledge, that was the first time that Morgan referred to Lisa by her name, and not simply as 'The Human.'

"However, this comes with a whole different set of rules."

Uh-oh. I don't think I was going to like this.

"You see, I have tolerated your companion because I honestly believed that she would either tire of what life with a ghoul would be like…"

Once again with the *'Hey, I'm standing right here!'* look. Morgan either didn't notice or—more likely—didn't care.

"…that, or she would end up dead. Seriously, your standard human never really fares well when becoming involved with the supernatural."

"Then why didn't you say something?" Lisa snapped.

"Excuse me, child, but I believe I have said things on many different occasions. And this most recent case is an example. I specifically warned Ava about involving you."

"I told her, but she said she—" I started to defend myself, but Lisa waved me off.

"How did your *pet* human die?" Lisa really put a nasty emphasis on that one word. I think she was tired of the games, too. I was beginning to wonder if maybe the wrong person had become the ghoul.

Morgan did not show any hint of emotion at that question. No surprise. But she did start talking. Big surprise.

"I was barely twenty when the Augustines came to my village…"

Holy crap! She is fixing to tell us some seriously personal stuff. I really have to focus.

"…when they spoke to mother, I was terrified. All my life I'd had this ability to…sense things. Lately, there had been a real surge in the growth of the new religion called Christianity since that very unpleasant incident in Jerusalem.

"People were hunting down anybody that they considered to be a witch. The entire supernatural community took quite a hit during that time. In fact, it was around then that most supernaturals began to go in to hiding.

"Every once in a while, one of them would show up and create a stir. There was actually talk early on of all the supernaturals coming together and simply eliminating the entire human race. Fortunately, cooler heads prevailed."

"Wait, you were around during the time of Jesus?" I'm sorry, but am I the only one who heard that little statement and didn't have some questions.

"That's really not important right now, Ava," Morgan scolded. "Lisa has asked a question, and I will grant her an answer this *one* time. So, if you don't mind…"

"Sorry," I whispered. Still, aren't *you* just a bit curious? I know that I am.

"So where was I?" Morgan shot me a dirty look.

"The Augustines had come to your mother and you were afraid because folks were hunting down witches," Lisa prompted.

"Wait a minute!" I snapped.

I had a sneaking suspicion that we were being played. If these so-called Augustines were searching for her *and* the crucifixion had just happened, her time line was way off. Probably didn't know that I went to Catholic School when I was in seventh and eighth grade, did ya? Well I did. And in the eighth grade we all went through Confirmation. It is one of a jillion ceremonies that they have in the Catholic Church. But the big part of that for me was choosing my patron saint. I picked Saint Augustine. Now my reasons may have had more to do with the fact that my great-grandmother lived in St. Augustine, Florida, but that is beside the point. Still, other than discovering that he is the patron saint of, among other things printers and brewers and sore eyes (I know, weird, huh?), I also know that he was born around the year 350 AD.

"How did an order named for somebody that still had a few hundred years to go before being born show up looking for you?" I challenged. "If this all happened around the time of the crucifixion, then St. Augustine doesn't come around for another few centuries."

"I applaud your apparent knowledge of history," Morgan said flatly. "And yes, the man that the Augustines eventually fell under the command of was not yet born when their order arrived in my village. At the time, they were simply known as The Order, but they have been Augustines for much longer, and therefore, that is how I refer to them. Do you have any more questions or comments, or may I finish answering Lisa's question?"

"No...go ahead." I made a little wave with my hand and tried not to look like a scolded child. What was it about Morgan? She had the answers for everything. Every single time we meet, I end up feeling like an absolute idiot. Still, I should probably pay attention; there might be a test later.

"...Lucinda and I even shared the same nurse. Her mother had died giving birth, something very common in those times. We basically grew up as sisters. She was the first person that I ever told about the strange things I could feel.

"When the Augustines took me, she cried. I promised that I would come back for her someday. They took me to Venice where I trained with others just like me. It seemed that the decision had been made to scatter the supernaturals all across the globe. We would be tasked as the mediator to handle their disputes.

"It was during this training that I learned how to focus my senses and locate any supernatural in an almost thirty mile radius. I also discovered that I could bind them to me if I chose—"

"Hold on!" I interrupted. "So I am *bound* to you? When did that happen? And what does that mean?"

"No, *you* aren't," Morgan said softly. "I have left you unbound intentionally. At first it was because I seriously doubted your ability to function. However, I soon realized that you could be very beneficial if left in your free state."

Now I was more confused than on the first day of math class. I am sure that all of this might make perfect sense to somebody, but I am so lost!

"Just sit down, Ava," Morgan said in an almost kind voice. I think I sat more out of shock. "All of this can come in time, but let me finish with Lisa. When this is all over with Adrianna, we can talk again…just you and I."

I nodded. Now all I had to do was keep from having my curiosity eat me alive until I had the chance to sit down with Morgan and get some answers.

"After my training was complete, I was to be sent to Bari, Italy. That would be my first district. Twenty years had passed and I was anxious to try out all that I had learned…"

Twenty years! Wow, and doctors think they have a lot of schooling! Damn, I'm doing it again. Maybe I could take one of those classes that supposedly teach you how to concentrate and focus.

"…during training, it was stressed that we leave our past behind. We were warned that there would be too much danger in our lives. Not all supernaturals were compliant, and we were tasked with putting our districts in order. Still, I desperately wanted to see my friend Lucinda.

"When I arrived, I barely recognized her. While I had maintained the same appearance as when I'd been taken away, she had aged. Years of hard living had taken a toll as her face was etched with lines and her mouth, which always had a laugh and a smile when we were girls, was now turned down in a near permanent frown. Still, when she saw me, she ran across and scooped me into the biggest hug…"

I tried to imagine anybody 'scooping' Morgan into a hug. That image just refused to take shape in my mind.

"…about her life mostly and what had happened in the village in my absence. It seemed that Lucinda had married, but her husband had died on a hunting trip. Two days later, her home burned down. From then on, she was seen as cursed and nobody would have anything to do with her. She begged me to take her with me.

"At first, I refused. I explained that I would be dealing with things that she might not understand. She reminded me of how she had always believed in me when I spoke of things I could sense. She said that she could help by caring for my home. I did not see the harm and eventually relented.

70

"When we arrived in Bari, I was met by a Templar. He immediately confronted me on my having a companion. I explained that she would be caring for my home in my absences. He said it was not his business, but he had a sad look that I did not understand at the time.

"My first task was to settle a dispute between three rival vampire factions. To make this long story short, one of the factions did not appreciate my efforts. One night they came and took Lucinda. The worst was yet to come—"

"What do you mean when you say they *took* her?" Lisa asked. "Didn't they just kill her?"

"That would have been too easy," Morgan said with a sigh.

This was the most emotion from her that I'd seen, and it was actually a bit unsettling. It would be like seeing the pilot of an airplane run out of the cockpit in hysterics and lock himself in the bathroom.

"They turned her, but then refused to feed her. I did not discover this until I was tasked with seeking out a revenant," Morgan explained.

I'd dealt with those before. They are like crazy vampires that are more animal than human.

"So you had to hunt her down and kill her?" I blurted. Morgan's face actually twitched. Honestly, I didn't mean to say anything. I couldn't help myself.

"Yes." That was all she said, but there was more in that word than I could ever express with a thousand.

The three of us remained in an uncomfortable silence for what seemed like forever. Finally, Morgan stood and approached Lisa. She put her hands on the girl's shoulders and leaned in close, whispering something in her ear that, even with my abilities, I couldn't hear. Didn't anybody ever tell her that it is rude to tell secrets?

Lisa listened, nodding a few times. Afterwards, Morgan simply walked out. I thought she was going to share something with me to help me take down this Queen of the Zombies!

As for Lisa, she got a serious look on her face and went to her room and closed the door, leaving me all by myself. Maybe I should get a dog.

Five minutes later, Lisa emerged with a carry bag and her pack. Imagine my surprise when my nails started to pop out. I thought that only happened when I was scared or really angry. Apparently my body can't tell the difference between upset and those other two.

"So you're leaving?" I finally asked when I felt that I could speak without my throat closing. I still was not sure about scertain aspects of my biology. Are ghouls are able cry? I had a feeling that I was about to receive a final confirmation on that theory.

"Just for a little while," Lisa said with a look on her face that reminded me a lot of that scene at the end of *Old Yeller* when the boy took the dog out to shoot him.

"Does 'a little while' have a date?"

"I'll be back when this thing with Adrianna is over."

"Why?"

"Because I won't let something happen that ends up with you having to kill me."

"So stay home!" I exclaimed. She didn't have to come, I would be totally fine with her staying home. That was way better than her up and leaving.

"And what about next time?" Lisa asked. "These things aren't going to get any easier."

"So what are you doing?" A tiny alarm bell rang in the back of my mind.

"I am going to listen to Morgan's advice," Lisa said as she headed for the door.

"What advice is that?" I tried to follow, but when she opened the door, the slightest glow in the sky was like a brick wall. I had no idea if it would kill me, but I already knew for a fact that it burned really bad. I stood just in the shadow of the door…helpless to do anything else.

That is when I discovered something new. Given certain conditions…as rare as they might be…ghouls *can* cry.

8

Don't Know What You Got ('Til It's Gone)

The rest of the day seemed to be endless. On more than one occasion, I found myself calling out to ask a question, only to have my voice echo around an empty home. What was most upsetting was the fact that I had always seen myself as an independent woman who needed nobody.

I went down to my basement for my evening meal, closing the door out of habit. I always shut it when I ate because I didn't think that Lisa would appreciate walking in to discover me chomping on a fresh corpse. I had even considered going so far as to have one of those lights installed like they had for darkrooms. If I was 'indisposed' then I could flip the switch. Lisa had been the one to veto that idea.

"I know what you do down there, but I'd just as soon not have a light acting as a reminder that you are eating a human."

"A *dead* human," I'd corrected.

"Not really comforting," she had said.

Perhaps that should have been my clue. We were very different. And maybe there was something to be said about not having a human around to worry about. Now I could concentrate on just being me; That Ghoul Ava.

73

I still wasn't all that well-versed on what being a ghoul was all about. With no Lisa to worry over or try and make time for, I could start seeking out more of my own kind. The biggest problem being that Morgan had said in one of our first meetings that ghouls were scarce; and she hadn't seen one in these parts before.

By the time night was fully on, I had managed to stuff all my real feelings in a nice little space and close the door. I was going to head back to Estacada tonight and deal with Adrianna. Or maybe I would see what she had to offer. I was basically a free agent. Hell, Morgan had the ability to bind all the supernaturals in her district and made the choice *not* to bind me.

That little sidetrack brought on a whole new batch of feelings—like being in gym class and being the last one picked. I know that not everybody can relate, but I've seen the people that go to those horror conventions or wait in line at the theater for the newest *Twilight* movie. Seriously, I am pretty sure that a lot of you know exactly what that whole 'being picked last' thing feels like.

So here I am, the newest supernatural in Morgan's district, and she doesn't even want to pick me for her team. I'm good enough to do her dirty work, but that's it? I don't think so. I wasn't that flat-chested, awkward little girl anymore.

I am Ava Birch and I am an ass-kicking ghoul…a force to be reckoned with. Maybe I would go to Estacada and bitch-slap Adrianna. I seem to recall that she smelled very yummy. Actually, I don't recall, I have to keep being told, but that doesn't mean anything. If she smells that good, then I am pretty sure she won't come with all the nasty drawbacks of a vampire. Which also made me wonder…what would a zombie taste like?

My mind went everyplace…and nowhere worth staying. Basically, I was a wreck. I realized before noon that Lisa had come to mean more to me than anybody else ever had in my life. Which begs the question; how pathetic was my life up to this point? I was a thirty-something woman when I changed, and I was now having my first real and meaningful relationship.

I started thinking about my past. I imagine if this was a

movie, then there would be some sappy song playing while all these scenes with fuzzy edges and a lot of slow motion played on the screen. The problem that I was coming up with was the fact that not even my mind could manufacture anything worth replaying.

Is it me, or has everything reached a point where nobody cares about anybody anymore unless there is a big disaster and a telethon? Here is a question. What are the first names of your neighbors...on both sides! What do they do for fun?

When I was little, there were all these shows on when I got home from school. I watched *The Brady Bunch* and *Bewitched* and *The Courtship of Eddie's Father* each afternoon while I waited for my mom to get home from her secretary job in some office with a boss that smelled like onions and dirty feet.

The life I saw on television is what I thought was waiting for me when I grew up. I never really clued in to the fact that my home was so far from all of that, yet I clung to this dream that every day would be an adventure to be wrapped up by the time I climbed into bed with my Mike Brady...my version, not the gay one on television. And no, I'm not calling him names, he really was gay. Seriously, I read that somewhere.

As I got older, I started to realize that things were not going to be like on television. For one, there was that whole thing about my flat chest, but it was lots of other things. And by the time I graduated, I didn't have a clue. So I drifted.

But it just seems that the last few years we have become more and more withdrawn as a society. That is why I was able to lie dead on my bathroom floor for a few days and nobody noticed. We really don't notice anything that is not put directly in front of us.

So I thought about Lisa. I thought about how I really hadn't appreciated her being with me until now...when she is gone. But through it all, it kept coming back to one thing. This all happened because of Adrianna, The Queen of the Zombies. Well I was going to fix her little red wagon.

And that was another thing! When I was little, we played with wagons and Barbies and regular stuff. Now, if it isn't run by a computer chip, kids look at it like it might try to steal their soul.

Rrrrinnng.

Hmm. Who could be calling me in the middle of the day? I guess anybody. That was one of the things that Lisa used to take care of before she up and left.

"Hello?" I answered on the third ring. Just in case it was Lisa, I didn't want her to think that I was sitting here waiting for the phone to ring and have it be her.

"What is wrong with your society?" a voice scolded.

Wasn't I just thinking about that? How funny. But this person was directing a question at me, perhaps I should answer. "And who is this speaking?"

"Ava, it's me…Adrianna?"

Oh, speaking of the bitch and most recent pain in my ass. "What are you talking about?" I had to ask since I really didn't know what she was talking about. I mean it could be an indictment on our public schools, or maybe the most recent property tax bond—although I doubted it was the last one. The Queen of the Zombies probably didn't pay taxes. Plus, the only reason I knew such a thing existed is because there was a commercial on television for it right this very second.

"Virgins."

I waited. I mean surely she had to have something bothering her other than virgins. And why would people be bothered by virgins? Seems to me that they don't fuck with anybody. See what I did there? The whole not fucking thing? Geez, I hate having to explain my jokes to people. They stop being a joke the moment that you have to explain them. From that point, they become a story problem.

"Are you there, Ava?"

Something about her voice bothered me more than normal. In fact, all I felt now was irritated by her existence.

"Get to the point, Adrianna," I snapped. After all, she called me for crying out loud.

"Doesn't anybody keep their legs closed in this morally corrupt society?"

"Having a hard time finding the virgin you need to make your unstoppable zombie horde?" I didn't bother hiding my sarcasm. In fact, if I may say so, I heaped on extra portions. I was having a crappy day, and it was largely in part to having encountered Adrianna.

"Well...yes," she said. After a really long pause, she continued. "But I believe the answer to my problems just showed up."

"What do you mean?"

But that question was lost to the phone line. She had hung up on me. How incredibly rude. Hmm, that reminds me, I wonder whatever happened to that girl from *Full House*. Everybody from that show still shows up from time to time...the anorexia twins never seem to go away...and Bob Saget. How did they ever become relevant? But that one girl with the cute little catch phrase. Once per episode, like it or not, she would spout, "How rude!" I wonder if people still ask her to say that like they used to bother that little Gary Coleman about that "What choo talkin' 'bout, Willis?" line. Do you think she ever wanted to climb into a clock tower and start picking off citizens?

Now I can't stop laughing. That's just great. I have a so-called Queen of the Zombies to nab, and all I can think of is the girl from *Full House* sitting on a ledge with a high-powered rifle, peeking through the scope as she slams another round into the chamber and pulls the trigger while screaming, "How rude!" What makes it even funnier is the fact that she stuffs a Twinkie into her mouth between each shot.

You know? I really do have an overactive imagination. These days, they call it ADD or ADHD. When I was little, they just said "Little Ava is a 'creative spirit' that needs to focus more on schoolwork and less on her magical world."

I went into my living room. It was still a few hours before the sun would go down. I had a few things I wanted to take care of before I drove out to Estacada to deal with that snotty little Queen of the Zombies. Great...now I am hearing an orchestra playing this dark little tune, "duh, duh, DUHHHHHH!" every time I think about her.

I may not have Lisa, but I am not some helpless damsel in distress. I have switchblade fingers and toes...and good old sharkmouth. All I'd seen from Adrianna was the ability to smell yummy and make me forget. Anybody who knows me at all can testify that that last trait is no big accomplishment.

9

Do You Really Want To Hurt Me

I hate surprises. Well, let me clarify that. If it is a set of diamond earrings, I love those. I've never been a flowers and candy sort of girl. Flowers die, and candy made me have to do ridiculous things like sit ups...and the most useless of all exercises: Jumping Jacks. Seriously, what the hell is Jack's problem? Let's totally take the part out of the equation where no sports bra that I'd ever found managed to keep the puppies in place. All a Jumping Jack does is let you feel which parts of you are jiggling more than they should. Basically...I hate Jumping Jacks.

But back to surprises.

Sitting on the hood of my brand new Corvette was a guy. You might be wondering if he was cute. Sure. He has a certain Brad Pitt thing working with his little bit of scruff and his sparkling eyes, but I think I may need to reiterate something. He. Was. Sitting. On. My. Corvette.

"You must be Ava," he said this like his butt was not leaving an imprint on the sweet, red paint of the hood of my Corvette.

"You must be—" And that was when the smell hit me. Chocolate cake dipped in Dumpster filth.

"My name is Jeremy Ames."

"You're a vampire," I spat. "And you are sitting on my Corvette!"

He looked down like he was noticing that most beautiful automobile for the very first time. Then he slid forward and stood up. I wanted to stake him right there.

But, Ava, you are probably saying, *he looks like Brad Pitt? You could dunk Brad Pitt in raw sewage and I'd still ride him like a roller coaster.* Did you miss the part about him sitting on my Corvette? Or that he *slid* off of it?

"I may not eat you," I snarled. "But I do know how to make your type turn into a little cloud of ash." I patted the bag at my side, the one that still had stakes and holy water and all manner of killing implements that removed pesky undead or your money back.

"Belinda said you were a real interesting sort," Jeremy laughed.

His fangs caught the light and flashed. If this were a movie, or one of those silly romance books, I would have found it 'strangely attractive' or some such nonsense. The only thing that found it was annoying.

"And what does that pain in the ass want?" I snapped as I shoved past the uncomfortably attractive—but still stinky—vampire. I rooted through my carry bag and found a crumpled tee shirt. I leaned in close and began removing the near-perfect butt print from the hood of my car.

"She has sent me to accompany you on your assignment," Jeremy said.

"I don't need, nor do I *want* help from one of her little toadies."

"She said that you would refuse." Jeremy came up beside me. "Missed a spot." He actually had the audacity to point! "But she told me to explain that Morgan insisted I join you now that you no longer have…" He stopped talking.

I looked at him and realized that not every vampire seemed to be able to hide their feelings. Jeremy looked openly cautious.

"Since you no longer…" Jeremy paused and seemed to consider what he was about to say, basing his caution on the obvious look of disapproval on my face. "And these are her words, not mine, so please don't do anything crazy."

Did I seem like the kind of person to do anything crazy? Did I fly off the handle over little things? And who was this guy to imply that I might be unstable.

"Just spit it out!" I growled.

"Since you no longer have your silly pet human," Jeremy said those words so fast that my brain had to add the spaces between each one; otherwise it would have just sounded like so much gibberish.

I stared at him for a long moment. Actually, I was waiting for my fingers and toes to do their thing. However, nothing happened. I would have to think on this more later, but for now, I was going off of the assumption that nothing Belinda said would matter to me one way or the other anymore.

"Do you have any idea what it is that I am doing?" I asked after taking one more look at my hood for any lingering butt prints.

"Not really," Jeremy said with a shrug. He reached inside the front left pocket of his much-too-loose-for my-liking jeans and pulled out a phone. "But it was important enough for Belinda to give me this."

"A phone?" I wasn't impressed. I had a phone. Hell, everybody had one.

"This one has a tracking program." Jeremy's fingers flew over it and he held up the display for me to see.

"So she wants to know where you are…whoop-di-frickin'-do!"

"You don't understand." Jeremy stuffed it back in his pocket. I couldn't be sure, but I thought that I saw a hurt look flash across his face. "She doesn't care where we go or what we do as long as we make our monthly tributes and don't end up on the news."

"So what you are saying is that Belinda isn't much of a hands-on type of leader?"

"That is putting it lightly," Jeremy grumbled. "When I moved here from San Diego thirty years ago, I thought I would have it better. But I guess Erma Bombeck is right."

"Who?" I opened my door and put my stuff inside.

"This lady who used to have a column in the papers…not that anybody reads the paper anymore…"

Great. In all the books and movies, these cute vampires show up and get all macho. They save the pretty girl or fight other vampires to defend her honor. They are badass dudes who sweep the girl off her feet whether she wants it or not. *I* get the sniveling philosophizer hung up on 'the way things used to be' or some such nonsense.

"Your point?" I gave him the 'hurry up' gesture with my hands.

"Just that Belinda never gives us a tracking phone. I honestly don't think that she would notice if we were gone until the dues went unpaid."

"Wait, you have to pay dues to her?" What kind of messed up situation was this? And I have read a few of those books now since Morgan said that some of them actually have nuggets of truth in them. I don't recall anybody mentioning membership fees. This might be interesting later, but right now, I had The Queen of the Zombies to deal with.

"…all of the Kiss leaders decided."

Damn, I guess Jeremy had been talking. Oh well, I really do have enough on my plate right now. The last thing that I need to be worrying about is vampire politics. I mean, I wasn't actually all that interested in regular politics, so the vampire's problems were really his own.

"If you are going, then get in."

I hopped in my car and allowed myself just a few seconds to bask in the comfort. Seriously, if this thing came with an option that gave vibrating seats, I would never need a man.

I glanced over at Jeremy who was dutifully fastening his seatbelt. He was either safety conscious…or has some doubt as to my ability to drive this baby.

Ladies, what in the world is wrong with men? I mean besides all of the really obvious stuff. They think they have the handle on everything. And if a lady gets in behind the wheel of a sports car, they act all crazy, like we don't belong. Same thing with motorcycles. Let a gal cruise down the highway on her hog and you'd think she was Lady Godiva for all the stares that she gets. I got news for you, just because we don't…doesn't mean that we can't. Seriously, boys, you can be replaced by a few inches of rubber and a couple of D-cell batteries, so I wouldn't be too cocky. Hmm…that was almost a pun.

As I pulled out into the street, I noticed Jeremy try to casually put his hands on the dashboard. *Fine…you want to have something to be afraid of, mister? Do any of you have the slightest idea what it feels like when the gas pedal hits the floor in the new Corvette?* I take back the comment about needing vibrating seats.

"Not much for being subtle, are you?" Jeremy yelled above Simon and the boys laying down their funky groove about a girl named *Rio*.

"What?" I batted my eyes and played the innocent. Of course, with my dark glasses on, I doubt he noticed.

"You always drive with this much anger?"

"How come when a guy drives fast, it is no big deal, but when a gal does it, it has to be about anger or being crazy?"

"I was talking about the gray skin." Jeremy touched my arm.

It was only a slight touch, but it gave me a tingle. His finger was cool and it only ran down my skin for the briefest of moments, but it felt great. I had this sudden thought that it had actually been quite a while since I'd had sex. Well, with a partner at least. Just because I'm a ghoul doesn't mean that I'm dead. Wait. Actually it does. But I still have my regular sex drive and all that jazz. I guess that might be confusing.

Wait a minute! a voice screamed in my head. This is not one of those weird 'paranormal romance' thingies. I am not going to get caught up in one of those. Like I said, I've read enough of those books. They always start out fine, but somewhere along the line they become all about sex. The lead female usually turns into a bit of a whore. Sure, she tries to play it off as being a 'strong, independent woman' as she hops from bed to bed, but we are all thinking the same thing. Right?

I yanked the wheel hard to the right and slammed on the brakes, skidding to a stop in the emergency lane. I took off my glasses and turned in the seat to give my full attention to the vampire beside me.

"I want you to pay very close attention," I said. "I have no idea why Belinda sent you. I am pretty sure Morgan is involved in this somehow—"

"You've met Morgan?" He asked it like somebody might do if you say you have met Jesus. And let me clarify that a bit. Not 'Have you found...?' but in the literal sense of actually *meeting* the real life Jesus.

"Of course I have," I snapped. I hated it when people interrupted me. "What's the big deal?"

"She only meets face-to-face with the upper echelon of the supernaturals in her district."

Now he was acting like *I* was Jesus. He was staring at me with these great big eyes that belonged on a Japanese anime character.

"Stop changing the subject!" I snapped. "Now, as I was saying..." *Damn. Now I couldn't remember what I was saying.* Well, at least until I noticed that he had a pretty wide chest and that his shirt was open. Then it hit me like a dose of Spanish Fly.

"This isn't some sort of hook up. Are you following me?" Jeremy nodded. "This is some sort of arrangement where you have been sent to spy on me or something. We won't be going all Meg Ryan and Tom Hanks. You understand what I'm saying?"

Once again Jeremy simply nodded. But I was pretty sure that I detected a smirk.

After another of my 'untouchable' glares, (you know the kind, ladies)... We've all been to the club and had some guy start giving us more than a casual glance. He is sporting his backwards baseball cap and has that hideous lump in his lower lip that hides a big dip of some sort of nasty chew. You know that no amount of alcohol is going to be enough. You pull out that one special look that makes their little wee-wees shrivel. Of course they will tell their buddies that 'she's probably a lesbo' or some such nonsense. Yeah, I used *that* look on him.

We rode in silence the rest of the way. To his credit, Jeremy sat there and even had the sense to tap along with my music. We were just taking the turn into downtown when the song *Fallen Angel* by Poison came on.

Now I have been known to hurt a few people's feelings in my day with my 'say it like it is' nature. One of my big—ain't that cute how I said 'one'?—pet peeves is when people who have no business singing along choose to do so. There are a few people that nobody should ever try to sing with: Geoff Tate from Queensryche, Rob Halford from Judas Priest, and Freddie Mercury from Queen. That last one isn't because he has such a crazy range, but simply because Freddie has the voice of an angel and deserves respect. Very close on my list is Brett Michaels from Poison. I just think he is dreamy and I have vowed that I will drop everything and be on the first plane when he kicks the bucket. His sweet little ass is mine...literally.

Sorry, I tend to drift off a little when I start thinking about Mr. Michaels. Anyways, most people who sing along in the presence of others have no business doing so. Jeremy started singing and I already had one in the chamber. My standard question is: "Hey, who sings this?" They usually are able to answer with the correct artist; in this case it would be Poison. I quickly follow that with: "Then maybe you should let them do it."

That never fails to shut them up. Oh sure, you get the 'hurt feelings' look, but at least you get to listen to your song. Am I right?

However, Jeremy started in and I was so taken by his voice that I drove right past that laundry and pizza strip mall location that I'd come to that first night. In fact, before I knew it, I was at the outskirts of town. Now before you get the wrong idea, Estacada is really small.

When the song ended, I hit the button on my stereo and brought up my song menu. I dialed up *Every Rose Has Its Thorn*. With as much casualness as I could muster, I continued to drive like I knew where I was going. Unfortunately, I think I passed the high school three times before the song was over.

"You lost?" Jeremy said as the song ended.

"Just trying to see if I can sense her," I lied.

I pulled into the parking lot and parked in front of the pizza place this time. I shut down my car and glanced over to Jeremy, who had the sense to still be sitting there like nothing was going on. I was absolutely not going to play another song for him to sing. Seriously, if he started in on *Something To Believe In*, my panties might very well end up on the floor.

Not a romantic comedy, not a romantic comedy, I started to chant in my head. Of course, if I just treat him like one of those coin-operated horses that used to be in front of the store, I could ride him once and call it good.

See? That's just the sort of thinking that starts sending things on the road to ruin. Pretty soon some werewolf with amazing abs will show up, and then the two will be fighting over me, but I will be so torn, because I truly love them both…

Blech!

You see how silly that all sounds? I mean it might be good for thirteen-year-old girls who have not been called 'slut' or 'whore' by everybody at school yet to think that it is perfectly normal to 'be in love' with two guys at once. However, I seem to recall society having an entirely different view of those sorts of things.

Being a girl is a lot harder than it looks. Sure, the guys all think we hold the strings…and for the most part we do. But it all starts with the anatomically impossible Barbie, continues with every single magazine that waits at the check-out aisle at the store, and is celebrated in the movies.

10

One Thing Leads To Another

Look at me getting all 'issue' oriented. You don't need me to tell you this crap. I bet you're wishing I would hurry up and just go to town on The Queen of the Zombies, aren't you? Well let me share something with you.

I bet a lot have you have seen that movie, *Ferris Bueller's Day Off*. Well, you know how he breaks away every so often to talk to the audience? That is what I'm doing here. Don't worry about Jeremy, he won't move until I take the pause button off of this story.

I have been digging in to the horror thing ever since Morgan explained that some of the stuff you read is actually based on reality. Even more interesting, this stuff goes on right under your noses, and most humans don't even realize it.

I guess the closest you have come is Bigfoot. Oh yeah, he's real, but we can talk about that later. But the thing I wanted to discuss is your impatience. You want me to hurry up and deal with Adrianna. Am I right?

Just think about it, if everybody stayed out of the water, *Jaws* would have been a pretty boring movie. Are you following me on this? No? Then let me try to be a bit clearer.

Have you ever been watching a movie and the bad guy is right there in the crosshairs of the hero? Only, instead of pulling the trigger, something happens and the bad guy gets away. Or maybe the bad guy has the good guy all tied up. He is going to kill him, but first he has to tell him his plan. During that little monolog, the hero manages to wriggle free and escape. Think about it; if he didn't, the movie would have only been twenty minutes long and you would all be complaining about being ripped off.

Now are you on the same page? I hope so. Yes, I want to get Adrianna just as badly as you want me to, but if I would have figured out that she was right across the street the first time I went to Estacada...or even if I could have blown her away when we met at Voodoo Doughnut Too (hmm...wish I still like regular food, a bacon maple bar would be yummy), well then this would be just another short Ava adventure. So sit back, pop some corn, and just hang out with me for a while. I'll get her, don't you worry. If not, then this is going to be one of the shortest book series ever. Now back to me and Jeremy sitting in the car.

"So what's the plan?" Jeremy asked.

"Plan?"

I don't know who he had been getting his information from, but I'm not much for planning. Besides, plans just lock you in to a set of actions. Then, when it all goes wrong, you are standing there wondering what to do next. Sorta like that whole playing dead idea if you are ever attacked by a bear. If that doesn't work, you are really going to have a hard time implementing a second option.

"You know," Jeremy prompted. He even did that whole thing where he rolled his hands at the wrists like that would kick start my brain or something. "Like we sneak in the back door or something?"

I started to giggle. I'm sorry, but once he said that, all I could think of was him trying to get in Adrianna's 'back door.' Maybe I'm wrong, but in our limited exposure to one another, she actually struck me as kind of prudish.

You ever sit someplace where there are a lot of people walking past and try to imagine them having sex? No? Oh, you absolutely have to do this. The next time you are out someplace by yourself, just take a seat on a bench and watch people as they go by. Now try to figure out if they are super freaky, or DMV boring. In fact, that was where I came up with this little game. I was standing in line at the local DMV for what felt like eternity.

"What's so funny?" Jeremy asked. Although, from the look on his face, I am guessing that it wasn't the first time he'd done so.

"You said back door," I chortled while attempting my really bad *Beavis & Butthead* impersonation.

At first he just stood there with a blank look. I was afraid I'd sprained his brain…until he smiled. Then, very slowly at first, he joined in on the laughing.

I guess it was a good thing that we hadn't just parked and gone into the pizza place to start asking the locals about anything strange going on in the woods. If we had, we would have totally missed the old man zombie stumbling out of the alley a block away.

How weird is that? A town as small as Estacada and they still have dirty little alleys. I know, totally weird. I mean, an alley is something you expect in someplace like New York or Chicago. You certainly would not expect to find one in a tiny logging community like this.

"What do we do with it?" Jeremy asked as we got out of the car and moved in for a closer look.

He had rushed up to the zombie as soon as he realized what it was. Only, once he got close and took in a good whiff, he became a giant sissy. He poked at it with his fingers and kept jumping back like he was afraid of the damn thing. The trouble with that whole reaction was the simple fact that the zombie didn't even seem to notice that he was there. It just kept on trudging across the street like nothing was happening.

As for me. Well, I was having an entirely different response. As soon as I got a sniff of that thing, my sharkmouth had come on in full force. It was chomping time!

Part of me really wanted to tear into this thing, but it seemed to be walking with such a purpose that my cat-like curiosity told me to follow it a while and see what happens. It turned down a narrow residential street. This is where some of my special abilities really started to come in handy. I could listen to all the surrounding houses. So far, most everybody was settled in and listening to the evening news. A few were already asleep, and one house made me blush…if ghouls blush that is. I know that I quickly redirected my attention away from that particular house as soon as I realized what it was that I was hearing. Okay…not *right* away, but pretty soon.

Then something happened that really got my attention. The left arm fell off of the zombie. Not wanting it to go to waste, yes I picked it up and snacked on it as I continued to follow. Jeremy, to his credit, stayed just a few steps away and didn't try to bother me while I ate.

I kept pace with the zombie as it made another turn. I was not all that surprised when the other arm fell off. Hey, you have popcorn, I get zombie arms.

However, I was surprised when the zombie stopped at a house that was sort of away from the beaten path. This place was little more than a run-down shack. The zombie, what was left of him anyway, walked up to the rusty fence and stopped at the gate. When it looked down, I imagine that was the first time it became aware that it no longer had any arms. By the way…they were dee-lish!

I was ready to move in and put this thing away when the door to the house opened and an old lady came out.

"That you, Horace?" she squawked. "Told you if you left with that eye-tal-yon gal that you could just stay gone."

Horace's only reply was a low moan. Well, at least I knew that Adrianna had been here. Not a lot of European women wandering around the streets of Estacada, Oregon. But the question now was, why here? Why these people in particular?

I stopped dead in my tracks; no pun intended. Although I do have to admit that was a pretty good one. Something about all of this suddenly made no sense at all. This Queen of the Zombies was bent on taking over the world. That part I don't really have a problem with. Granted, I don't understand it, but I guess it must simply be part of her nature. What I was totally at a loss to explain was why she would come to this place. And not that I have anything against my beautiful Pacific Northwest, but nothing really major when it comes to world events happens here. In fact, Seattle would be a much more appropriate setting for somebody bent on taking over or wiping out the world.

Estacada, Oregon is someplace I am willing to bet none of you have heard of in your life. Most of the folks who live in Oregon probably have no idea where this place is.

"Go back in your home, Betty," a voice spoke from the shadows.

I felt a slight breeze to my left. Jeremy had vanished. As for me, I was standing in the shadow of a tall hedge. One more step and I would have been in the flickering glow of the streetlight. Sometimes it pays to be lucky.

I watched Adrianna step into that streetlight's glow. She was wearing all black and looked sickeningly sexy. The outfit seemed to have been poured over her body. Not one little roll or bulge. Where is the fairness? Her hair was pulled back in a pony tail that barely reached past the base of her neck. To put it bluntly, she looked amazing.

"Who's there?" Betty snapped. "Sounds like that trashy little tramp that came and took my Horace?"

"I don't want you hurt, Betty," Adrianna said with surprising softness. "Go inside...now."

The zombie, Horace I have to assume, let out another moan. I saw this woman Betty stop in her tracks. She had actually been just about to return inside when she heard that pitiful sound.

"What have you done to my Horace?" Betty snapped. She reached inside her door. I was expecting a gun.

That is another thing about my beloved Pacific Northwest. If a zombie outbreak were to ever happen. I would give my state even money on the odds for survival—us and probably Texas.

Instead, she came out with a walker. She plucked the eyeglasses that hung from a chain around her neck and pushed them up on her nose with what I imagine must be considered defiance. Betty wasn't taking no crap from Adrianna. I expected Adrianna to blow up or something. I expected her to cop that smarmy attitude that she used with me when we met. Instead, she walked up to Horace and placed her hand on his forehead. The zombie dropped like somebody had just pulled the plug.

"Betty, please go inside, I will explain everything to you inside." Her voice was almost kind, that was not at all what I expected.

Tell her to kiss your wrinkly behind, Betty, I thought. I waited for that cantankerous old woman to lay into Adrianna like nobody's business. Instead, she turned and walked back inside. The rattling slam of the screen door followed a second later. This was not my night for guessing how people would react.

"Ava," Adrianna called into the darkness.

"Seriously?" I spat.

"I don't have time for you right now." Adrianna turned and looked right at me. I guess that's what I get for thinking that I am so unique and special. Perhaps when dealing with humans that was the case, but not when dealing with other supes.

"So you've known I was here the whole time?" I asked as I stepped out of the shadows.

"Yes, and your little vampire friend, too."

"Figures you would practically quote the Wicked Witch of the West," I grumbled.

"You shouldn't be able to do that," Jeremy said with way too much awe in his voice as he stepped off the roof of a house across the street.

"Met a lot of Zombie Queens have you?" Adrianna dismissed Jeremy with one hand and turned her focus to me. "And perhaps you were not clear when we parted ways. You and I are now set against the other. You have chosen to side with whoever is so recklessly in charge of this area."

Recklessly in charge? Morgan would love that…if I survived this encounter long enough to share that little tidbit.

"Can I call for a momentary truce?" I asked. Hey, it couldn't hurt.

"This is not really a good time," Adrianna sighed. She glanced down at the crumpled body at her feet, and then at the door that Betty had vanished through.

"Let me ask one question and I will leave you to whatever sick and twisted thing you have going on here," I offered.

"If you do me one favor, I will answer one question," Adrianna replied. The problem is, she came back with that way too fast for comfort. To say that I didn't trust her was a huge understatement.

"Don't get me wrong—" I started, but Adrianna was seriously impatient and cut me off.

"I told you that I don't have time for this, Ava," she snapped. "Either take the deal or leave."

That was kind of rude. Plus, it totally left out the possibility that just maybe we were going to have to fight it out right here and now. I mean, it was obvious that she was doing zombie stuff. There was no denying that one lay at her feet right this very minute.

My job, as assigned by Morgan, had been to come out here and deal with the zombie threat if one existed. I could now safely confirm that zombies were in fact wandering about the town of Estacada. Okay…it was only one, but it had to start someplace, right?

My quandary was still the whole 'why here' question. I will admit that I would probably never be nominated for detective of the year. However, I could find no logical reason why Adrianna would come all the way out to such a remote location from wherever she'd been kept imprisoned to kick off her latest attempt at wiping out the world.

In the end, I decided that it was unlikely that we could be standing on another of those thing-a-ma-jigs that bound us like at Voodoo. If her request was too unreasonable, I could just refuse and walk away. What would happen? She would hate me more? She would want to kill me? Twice?

"Okay, what is the favor?" I asked.

I was expecting something really terrible. In fact, I was already trying to figure out which way to run when I changed my mind. Let's face it, I still didn't know what sorts of powers this chick was packing. I already knew that she could erase herself from my memory and raise zombies. Although, from what I'd seen, she was not all that good at the latter.

"I need you to dispose of this," she pointed to the crumpled and armless figure at her feet.

"You want me to dispose of…mmrglllph?" I asked, not entirely sure of what her definition of dispose might be. I knew what mine was…stupid sharkmouth. How was I going to ask my question like this?

"Yes, and quickly." Adrianna didn't seem to have a problem with the way in which I would be disposing of her failed attempt at creating a zombie.

Have you ever watched the news when they show the newest little creature born at the zoo—especially the chimps. Sometimes they are really shy and timid when they deal with their handlers. They sneak forward, grab whatever food is offered and then scurry back to what they consider a safe distance.

I imagine that is a pretty accurate description of how I snatched up the old man's body and then quickly moved out of arms' reach. Adrianna didn't seem at all interested in me, though. And I went to town.

"Now, hurry with your question, I have something to do."

"Why here?" That seemed simple enough. Of course, without the *ju-ju* or mojo thing, I had no idea how much truth I would be getting. I already knew that Adrianna was not that interested in sharing information with me.

"Haven't you figured it out yet, you silly ghoul?" she laughed. The thing was, it wasn't one of those 'laugh with me' type laughs. This was definitely an 'at me' type of laugh.

"Maybe I just want to check my facts," I retorted as I wiped the last bit of ghoul drool from my chin. To his credit, Horace was pretty tasty. I had expected something far more stringy. And when I burped, I got a distinct aftertaste of whiskey.

"I doubt that." Adrianna opened the screen door that Betty had vanished through. "However, I will answer your question." She let the door shut at her back and turned to face me.

Hmm, this must be a doozy, I thought.

"My ancestors left the country shortly after I came into my powers. Whether out of fear or some other reason, I have no idea. Through whatever bizarre set of circumstances the Fates have spun, the bloodline is here."

I had to take a few seconds to process what she had told me. I guess I never really got into tracing my ancestors. Sure, I see those commercials for the genealogy sites, but I just never cared. Just my luck, I would discover that I am from a long line of waitresses and bar maidens that have had their asses grabbed and pinched over the centuries.

"So these are you great-great-however-many-times-over grandparents?" I asked.

"Something like that," Adrianna said with a nod.

"So you came here to find your family?" I wasn't sure I was seeing the big picture. In fact, if my history tells you anything…I barely see what is directly in front of me.

"That is another question," Adrianna said with a dismissive wave of her hand. With that, she turned her back on me and went inside.

I considered going after her. After all, she had turned an old man into a zombie and now she was inside with the wife. She claimed that they were relatives. I didn't see what that might have to do with anything. I just knew that I was missing something.

"Maybe we should go." Jeremy had my arm.

I snapped out of it and glanced at the vampire. Then I felt a wisp of something brush across my skin. My brain felt all funny, also, I wasn't sure, but I thought I might have eaten something that was having a strange effect on me.

"Where in the world are we?" I looked around and could not recognize a thing. That couldn't be good. Do ghouls sleepwalk?

"C'mon, Ava," Jeremy urged, tugging on my arm.

I heard something and glanced at the rickety house that I was standing in front of. Something in the back of my brain tried to break loose, but just that quick, it was smoothed over and I was back to being confused again.

"Wow," was all Jeremy said. He took my hand and led me back to my car.

My head started to swim, and it took me a few seconds to

realize what the problem might be. Although I didn't see how that could be possible.

"You better drive," I said, digging through my carry bag for my keys.

I had enough experience with this particular sensation to know it exactly for what it was: I was drunk. I had no idea how it had happened, but I was 'Last Call' drunk. In other words, it felt like I'd been at the club since the doors opened sucking down the booze that some guy had given me all night with the hopes that I would be putting out. I have to confess…that worked way more times than it ever should.

I found the keys and tried to hand them to Jeremy, but apparently I tried to put them in the wrong hand. To clarify, of the three Jeremys that I was currently seeing, I handed my keys to the one on the left. That one turned out to be a mirage or something.

I tried to bend down and pick up my keys, but was faced with a new dilemma: two sets kept swirling back and forth and changing places with each other.

"This can't be good," Jeremy muttered as he bent down and grabbed my keys on the first try!

"Well aren't you just special," I said while admiring the view of what I discovered were surprisingly firm buns. I say 'surprisingly' only because I have no idea how I had not noticed them before.

I reached out to grab a set, hoping desperately that I got the real ones this time. Nope. And now I was sitting on the ground. Actually, sitting is not the right word. I was on my side, sorta, and leaned up against my car.

Yikes! Had I scratched my beautiful new baby? I ran my hands over the shiny red surface and put my face really close so I could see. It looked okay, but I was amazed at how cool the polished red metal felt against my cheek.

"Up we go," Jeremy said as he reached under my arms and pulled me to my feet.

Now I was face to face with this very cute, and for some reason, very serious looking, vampire. I ran one finger under his smooth chin and was thrilled that I got the right one. His face was so close to mine that I didn't actually see two, but the one I did see was all wavy and shimmery.

Now just a second! I know what you are thinking. I said shimmery. I did not say sparkly. I have no idea why that whole thing started, but vampires do not sparkle or glitter…or whatever. So don't start accusing me of saying something that I didn't.

But back to the curiously attractive vampire. I leaned in close and kissed his cheek.

That was all it took. I shoved him away from me and stumbled to the curb where I leaned over and hurled. Hey…I didn't know that ghouls could puke either, so this is news to both of us. A glance over my shoulder proved that it was a surprise to Jeremy as well.

I looked down at the slurry that was all over that drainage grate. I was pretty sure that I could make out most of a liver and all of the heart. I got news…it did not taste nearly as good the second time.

My head was still spinning, but it seemed that I was at least over the puking. I staggered back to the car where Jeremy had remained with the cutest look of confusion on his face. I wiped my mouth with my sleeve and tried to smile.

"Are you going to be okay?" Jeremy asked.

"I think so…why?"

"Because you have a strange look on your face."

So much for my 'sexy eyes' look. I guess when they are solid black, it is difficult to make them sexy. I tried another approach.

"You wanna fuck?"

"Umm…"

That is never a good response. You see, I have discovered in all my years with men that they are pretty much in the mood twenty-four hours a day. They could be on their death bed and would want to give it one last go 'round. Seriously, ladies, next time your man is sick. Get him into bed and slither under the covers. A lick and a tickle and the little soldier is ready for duty.

"Are you sure that you are in any condition—" he began.

"My condition?" I snapped. "I'm not pregnant. I just ate something that obviously did not agree with me. I'm fine now, and I have noticed you sneaking a few looks here and there…" I sniffled big and dabbed at my eyes. The fact that there weren't actually any tears was irrelevant at the moment.

"Ava," Jeremy said in a soft voice as he stepped close and wrapped his arms around me, "I just mean that you might be poisoned or something. In fact, if I didn't know any better I would say that you are drunk."

"Can supernatural beings get drunk?" I asked with another big sniffle as I burrowed my face into Jeremy's chest. Oops, big mistake. Remember that whole thing about vampires smelling like chocolate cake frosted in filth? I turned my head to the side and tried to suck in some clean air in hopes that it would keep me from yakking all over him.

"I know that vampires get a version of it from over-indulging in fresh blood. It is what makes them sloppy. A blood-drunk vampire is not as diligent in tidying up his or her mess. That is why we usually feed in groups."

"Like a designated driver?" I tried to fight back a giggle.

"In a way, I guess."

This was some of the worst foreplay in history. I did the only thing I knew to do. Yep, I reached down and grabbed it.

"Whoa!" Jeremy yelped like he'd been shot…or staked.

"I take that as a no," I huffed and pushed away.

It would figure, after all the books and movies, I had come to the assumption that vampires had this super libido. Either this was one of the myths and misconceptions, or I was not the type of girl that Jeremy found attractive.

"It's not that, Ava." Jeremy put his hands on my shoulders. "But I don't think that Belinda would be all that happy about it."

"Screw her!" I growled and jerked away. Then a thought came like a bolt of lightning. "Or is that what might be the problem? Are you and her doing the nasty?"

"Me and Belinda?" Jeremy had the sense to sound more put off by that notion than he had about the idea of having sex with me. "Not hardly. She would never stoop to having sex with another vampire…at least not one of her subjects."

This was probably all really good material. I am sure I would like to delve deeper into it later, but at the moment, I had an itch that needed scratching.

I pulled away from Jeremy and staggered towards the pizza place. With my exceptional hearing, I could hear a few people in there having fun. The sound of pool balls clacking against one another could be heard along with at least a handful of male voices.

I finally found the actual doorknob and went inside. If Jeremy followed…fine. If not, I didn't really care. Except for the part where I'd given him my keys, but that was a problem for later.

The place was actually surprisingly clean. I guess I was expecting something seedy and dingy. After all, I was in Estacada. Sure enough, a trio of guys were over at the pool table, They had a few pitchers of beer on a table nearby.

A quick look around revealed that there were two employees behind the counter. One was a great big guy with a ridiculously small tie that rested awkwardly on the enormous gut straining against the buttons of his brown checkered shirt. The girl behind the counter had some serious teen acne going on. I wondered if she had seen those commercials for all those face cleansers or not.

At a booth sat a young man and what I had to assume was his date. They were leaning against each other whispering. Since I have exceptional hearing, I heard the joke. To be honest, she laughed a little too hard. It wasn't that funny.

One table had a cluster of women and several empty carafes of wine. They were much louder than the guys playing pool. A quick look had me wondering who might be the designated driver because they were all pretty well sauced. Even worse, they kept making outwardly lewd comments directed at the three guys at the pool table. If they could hear what was being said in response, they might have shut up and slinked out like whipped dogs.

"Check her out," one of the guys hissed as I took a seat in

the corner and pretended to care about the heavy plastic menu that was stuffed between a half-empty parmesan cheese shaker and a napkin holder.

Yay for me and my hearing! I thought.

"Dude…is she gray?" another asked.

Crap, I hadn't bothered with airbrushing. In fact, with Lisa gone, I doubted that I could do a very good job anyways. She had been the one to practice until she got it perfect. Bless her heart, she had gone down to the basement and practiced on the bodies I brought home for dinner.

Now I was sad. If there is a cure for the female sex drive, it is depression. Back in my human days, feelings like this usually ended in a trip to the store in my slippers and baggy sweats. I knew the shortest route to the Ben & Jerry's ice cream parlor.

"…maybe she is from overseas," one of the guys was saying.

"And what country has gray people?" another quipped.

"Marty, have you seen her rack? That chick is sporting some serious sweater meat," the one questioning the possibility of my overseas origin pressed.

I didn't know whether to be flattered or offended. I'd heard my breasts referred to by a number of nicknames. This was the first I'd heard the phrase 'sweater meat.'

"Maybe she has some kind of skin condition…like Michael Jackson," the third, and up to this point, silent one, suggested.

"Dude, Michael Jackson was just a freak," the one who had pointed out my gray complexion retorted.

"Yeah, but he still put out some great music…until *Bad*. Then he just sort of fell off," the one called Marty offered.

"Sorta like Stephen King after *It*," the third said with a nod as he leaned over the table and sunk one of the striped balls into the corner pocket…along with the cue ball.

"Ten bucks says you can't get her number, Rocky," Marty challenged.

"Ten and you pay the beer tab," the Stephen King fan with the unfortunate name of Rocky countered. Seriously, what is wrong with people? It's like there should be a rule now banning people from naming their kids. They never seem to get it right. I think the nurses at the hospital should do it. It would prevent the dearth of Haleys, Brittanys, and Jordans. Also, children would no longer be forced to carry on some tired old family name.

In high school I had a friend named Eugene. Now this was in the Eighties when the only people named Eugene were clones from *Revenge of the Nerds*. The thing about this particular Eugene was that he had perfect hair, dreamy blue eyes, and the ability to catch just about anything thrown to him by our mediocre high school football team's quarterback.

I dated Eugene for a few months my junior year. He was so sweet, but I just could not keep from giggling when I would whisper his name while we were making out. That is a real mood killer, let me tell you. Even for a high school boy with overactive hormones, having your girlfriend giggle when you are trying to move towards second base can send the little soldier back into the foxhole.

I asked him what his middle name was, figuring that maybe I could start using that under the guise of calling it a pet name. It was Herbert. Yeah, that's what I thought as well…not much help.

I looked up to find the one called Rocky standing over my table. His bluster and bravado seemed to still be back with his beer and his buddies. Either that or he thought it was cute standing over me, twisting a napkin in his hands like he was wringing the neck of a chicken.

"Care to join my friends and me in a game of pool?" he asked.

Now that is actually a pretty good approach. I gave him points for that. Instead of trying to isolate me from the herd and move in for the kill, he was urging me to join in and have some fun. That could imply that he was not assuming anything. The problem I had was that I was not in the mood for small talk. I simply wanted sex.

So, I can hear some of the guys reading this saying, "What a bunch of crap! Women don't think that way. That's a guy thing." Okay, I will grant you that it is not probably nearly as common for us ladies as it is for you fellas, but believe it or not, sometimes we do actually get that way. Don't believe me? Okay, well if you have a gal pal, you know…the kind that you can talk about all kinds of stuff with and not worry about it? Then ask her. I got news for ya, boys…y'all don't have the market cornered when it comes to horny.

Damn, I must have been daydreaming again because now Rocky was kinda squirming. I really need to work on that.

"Sounds like fun," I said. "But…"

What is it with guys? They hear a 'but' and they immediately just assume that it is about to become a rejection. Rocky's almost cute smile had already started to slide off his face. I had to get the next sentence out before he turned and walked away.

"I am actually just looking to score," I said in a rush.

Rocky might not be such an inappropriate name after all. He got this confused look on his face. After literally scratching his head, he replied, "I think there is this one guy who hangs out at The Lumberjack Tavern, he might have some stuff—"

Great, I was going to have to spell it out for him.

"Sex, you idiot!" I may have said that a bit too loud, because both of his pool playing buddies' heads popped up like those cute little Meer cats in *Meercat Manor*. Also, the really loud and drunk ladies got strangely quiet. It was right about then that I realized that there was no juke box or anything playing.

A second later, the door to the pizza place opened and in came Jeremy. He scanned the room and homed in on me. I wasn't sure, but I thought he looked angry for just a second.

He bee-lined for me and stepped past Rocky like he wasn't even there. "Ava, there you are," he said with this super fake laugh like we were meeting at some sort of social gathering at Martha's Vineyard.

Now I should probably say that I have never actually been to Martha's Vineyard. To be honest, for the longest time, I thought it was named for Martha Stewart. I just have this image of these obnoxiously preppy people with names like Biff, Tad, and Muffy all sipping wine and mocking the poor. An entire island made up of the people like the ones that were so mean to

Dan Aykroyd in *Trading Places*. Not the two old geezers, but those turtleneck wearing toads with his girlfriend at the country club who turned on him so fast.

"...talking to the lady, pal," Rocky was saying to Jeremy.

"And now you are finished," Jeremy replied. He didn't make a threatening move or gesture, but I could hear something in his voice that screamed danger. Apparently Rocky was deaf.

"Maybe you want to discuss this outside," the silly human challenged. I saw his two friends set down their pool cues. So this was not going to be a very fair fight. For the humans, I mean.

I could almost smell the testosterone in the air. Hmm, do guy vampires have testosterone? I know they are supposed to be a bunch of horn dogs for the most part, if you believed even half of what you read, but maybe they had a different chemical that drove their lusty side.

One thing led to another, and pretty soon we were all standing outside the pizza place. Jeremy hadn't said much. Most of the ruckus was coming from the three amigos. The real curiosity came when the table full of older ladies followed the little procession.

"So maybe you want to take the first swing?" Rocky had moved right up into Jeremy's face. To his credit, Jeremy remained silent. I mean, he was showing restraint...right? Please tell me that not only did I get the only vampire lacking a sex drive, but I also got the coward of the bunch.

"Just bust his face, Rocky!" Marty urged.

"Less talking, more punching," the one I still didn't know the name of added.

As for the gaggle of ladies, something about them drew my attention. They were not yelling or carrying on anymore. They were simply watching. I scanned their faces and saw something in their eyes that made me wonder. Then one of them noticed me watching and whispered to the bunch.

One problem at a time, Ava, I told myself.

"You were a pretty big man inside," Rocky was saying. He kept poking one meaty finger in Jeremy's chest as he spoke.

I noticed a couple of things during that little interaction; the first being that Rocky was poking really hard. The second thing, and perhaps more important, was that Jeremy was not registering that contact at all. What I mean is that his body was not budging. If that guy had been poking me that hard, I would have fallen over. Of course that was what started this whole thing…me wanting him to poke me that hard. See what I did there?

"Go back inside," Jeremy said. At first, I thought I had imagined it. His voice was so quiet that it took a few seconds for me to realize that he'd spoken at all.

"Or what?" Rocky challenged, confirming that Jeremy had finally decided to speak.

In a flash, Jeremy had Rocky by the neck and pinned to the wall of the building. Oh yeah, that whole vampire speed is pretty scary stuff. There was a gasp from everybody, even the curiously quiet ladies that continued to watch with a very peculiar inquisitiveness.

"Holy shit," Marty gasped, taking a few steps back and actually bumping into the ladies who, in another interesting twist, shoved him forward like they were offering him up for slaughter.

The guy whose name I still didn't know took a much different approach. He charged Jeremy. I was going to say something, but before I could open my mouth, Jeremy simply reached out with his other free hand and caught the guy by the throat. In one way-too-easy move, he brought the other man around and pinned him to the wall beside his buddy. Yeah. Now he was holding two men against the wall by the throats; both of them had their feet dangling a few inches off the ground.

"I am only going to say this once more," Jeremy hissed, and this time, he let just a little bit of fang slip out. I don't know if it was intentional or not, but I know that both of those guys got so wide-eyed that they each suddenly resembled Boston Terriers or Pugs…or whatever those little bug-eyed dogs are. Then the nameless guy went a step further.

The sound of liquid splashing on the sidewalk was amplified by the silence. I actually felt sorry for the guy. Weeks from now, when this pack of yokels started to retell this little incident, they would probably reshape it to make themselves sound braver and more in control. However, that one guy was not going to be able to dismiss the fact that he had just peed himself. Maybe he would blame it on the beer.

"I am going to set you down now," Jeremy said in an almost pleasant tone. "Am I going to have any problems?"

Two heads shook vigorously. Jeremy didn't actually set them down. He sort of just dropped them.

"Ava, get in the car," Jeremy whispered in my ear. I watched the three guys huddle around each other and overheard snippets of what was being said.

"...gonna let that go?"

"...all three of us at once!"

"...and get away with it!"

Okay, so maybe it was time to go. I hopped in the car, but I took one last look at those ladies. They were all still just staring at us. There was something very weird about them.

As we pulled out and headed to the freeway, Jeremy glanced in the rearview mirror.

"I really hate faeries," he spat.

It took me a moment to realize that he was not being derogatory towards those three yahoos. He meant those women. Like I said earlier, one thing at a time, Ava.

11

(I Just) Died In Your Arms Tonight

We drove in silence. I was feeling a little woozy. The drunk feeling was turning into that in-between state where you start to know that you are going to have a killer hangover in the morning. Of course, my problem was that I didn't need sleep. That meant I would be awake for the entire glorious event.

The engine switched off and the two of us sat in silence as the garage door slowly closed behind us. I was feeling a bit awkward. One of the beauties of jumping into the sack with somebody when you are blotto is that usually both of you are suffering from the same degree of over-consumption. When you wake up next to some snoring oaf of a man, you slip out very carefully, put on the minimal amount of clothing that you can in order not to be arrested for indecent exposure, and then, with panties tucked in your purse, you exit.

When Jeremy leaned across my car and kissed me, I think it took me a second to realize just what exactly was going on. Unfortunately, I almost threw up in my mouth a little bit. Vampire kisses taste a lot like they smell. There was this rush of yummy, and then an aftertaste of pure nasty.

I gagged and he jerked away. I gave him an apologetic look, and once again we were sitting in uncomfortable silence. I had a thought.

"Look, can I ask you a question?"

"Sure, I guess."

"Did you do that because you wanted to, or because I guilted you into it?"

Jeremy sat quietly for a few seconds. That had me just a bit worried. Finally, he turned in the seat and faced me.

"I don't do anything out of guilt. Actually, one of the worst parts about being a vampire is that you lose all of your humanity over time."

I considered those words. That might make Belinda easier to understand. I would still hate the rude little bitch, but I might at least have a better understanding of what drives her.

"Do you think any person could continue to kill indiscriminately? Granted, we have become so much more than we were, but we still have ties to our humanity. Like, if we enjoy music, we still enjoy it as vampires. So there remains a lifetime of human influence in our minds. However, over time, our ability to feel actual emotion dies. So, no...I do nothing out of guilt."

That was a pretty good explanation. So now I could check something off the list. Unfortunately, what I still did not know was why he *did* kiss me.

"I find you appealing to the eyes, Ava."

I guess that is vampire speak for 'I think you're pretty.' I would take it.

"I would like to pay a visit to you when we are not tasked with stopping The Queen of the Zombies. Perhaps we can find a way to enjoy each other's company."

"Do you mean sex?" Hey, a girl has to ask.

"I mean that, yes. But I also mean perhaps getting to know each other better. I know nothing of you at all, but in just this short time, I find that you fascinate me like nobody I have ever met."

I did not care if he smelled or tasted like a steaming pile of doggy poo...my panties were coming off and he was in for the ride of his life.

"Okay," I leaned close and tried not to breathe through my nose, "we are going to my room now. You can't make an omelet without breaking eggs...or something like that. This is happening. We will just have to find out how."

Seriously, ladies…you know what I am talking about here, right? You know that first time with a guy when you absolutely want it to be perfect. And it just never is. He is so excited that the pistol fires too soon, or you just can't get comfortable. Maybe he isn't used to a girl with really long hair, so he keeps getting tangled in it, or pulling it.

Don't get me wrong. A good hair pull can be really hot, but there is a difference between getting your hair yanked and tugged versus having him wrap it in his hands and using it to pull your head back so he can sink his teeth into your neck or kiss you in that really rough way that gets that certain shiver…

Hmm, that may just be me. I might have shared too much. Oh well, the bottom line is that the first time often leaves a bit to be desired. And before you guys get *your* panties in a bunch. Maybe it is time to let you in on a little secret. No, the Earth doesn't move every single time. It is nothing against you, it is just that you guys are microwave ovens and we are more like crock pots. And don't think I didn't hear you when you changed the word 'crock' to the word 'crack'. You aren't that clever.

"…do that a lot don't you?" Jeremy asked with a lopsided smile on his face. It was in that very moment that I realized who he reminded me of. He looked like a really young Harrison Ford. Not even the one from *Star Wars*. I'm talking *American Graffiti* era.

"Do what?" I hated that I had to ask. That meant that I was doing it again.

"Space off into your own little world," Harrison…I mean Jeremy said.

"I may have issues with paying attention," I admitted.

"No…you go into a world all your own," Jeremy said with a chuckle.

"Look," not that this wasn't all cute and amusing, but Ava want nookie, "are we going to do this or not?"

"I would love to…" I heard the 'but' before he even said it, "…but the sun will be up very soon."

"I have a safe room. I don't like it on my skin either," I said.

"And when you say soon…"

"One of the abilities of a vampire is to be able to feel the arrival of the sun. It sets off a little warning bell in our system so we can get to ground or back to our lair if time permits."

"So how long do we have?"

"Sadly, only about forty minutes."

I laughed. You men are so funny the way you over-exaggerate your prowess. Now I have been with guys who can go again real soon after completion. And then there are the ones who can spend some serious time 'down under' if you know what I mean. However, do you know what the AVERAGE amount of time it takes a man to actually finish once he starts dipping the pickle? Two and a half minutes! Yeah…that is the average…

"But wait a minute there, Ava!" some of you guys are arguing.

Sorry, fellas. You can't argue with science or biology. Don't believe me? Look it up. Or how about this, next time you are in the act, pay attention to the song playing. Still the same song when you finished? How sad for you. Now back to Jeremy.

"But if we are going to do this—" he was arguing, "I will require more than just forty minutes."

"Look, I am not suggesting that you aren't an absolute stallion in the bedroom," *a little flattery goes a long way in this department, ladies*, "but this first time doesn't have to be something magical. Honestly, it would probably help to get it out of the way."

"Not holding out much hope of it being enjoyable?" I saw that hurt puppy look that you guys can get when we ladies are not actively stroking your ego.

"I just know that the first time can be awkward. Let's get it out of the way so that we can really enjoy the next go 'round."

"And not a hopeless romantic either, I see," Jeremy grumbled.

"Nope. Just mostly hopeless." He was wasting time. "Listen, Jeremy, neither one of us are virgins here. We've done the horizontal mambo before. I say we hop-oh in the sack-oh and see what happens."

"But you are aware that I have told you the sun is coming up soon."

"Yep."

"And you know what happens to a vampire when the sun rises?"

He had me there. I guess I assumed that they crawled into their coffins or whatever and waited for sunset. I gave a shrug.

"We die, Ava."

"But you are not alive." That seemed like a logical retort. If I was up to speed on our supernatural status, neither vampires nor ghouls were technically alive. I didn't need to breathe, but could do so if I thought about it. My heart didn't beat. I guess I figured that vampires were in the same boat.

"No," Jeremy sighed and sat back in the driver's seat.

Great, this was eating into valuable time and I really was starting to feel a rise in my sexual frustration. If I had to finish this off alone, I was going to be rather cranky when he saw me next.

"When the sun comes up, it is like a giant off switch in all but the most powerful vampires," Jeremy explained.

"So vamps like Belinda?"

"I wouldn't know for certain, but since she is the Queen of the Kiss, I would have to assume she is strong enough to resist if the need arises."

You know what they say about assumptions. Perhaps that would be something I could find out later. Not that I was planning on taking out the bitch, but if it ever came down to her or me, it would be nice to know the weaknesses of the enemy.

"...and we just shut down. So not only is that an extremely vulnerable position to be in, but some folks find it rather disturbing." Oh yeah, he was still talking.

"Well, in case you have missed the memo, I am not exactly human," I said with a smile that I hoped could get him to get his butt out of the car and up to my room.

"Yes, but if we are going to do this, I didn't want you to be surprised if I didn't want to talk or cuddle after. And I will be totally incapacitated until sunset."

Okay, I thought, *so you are a guy with the perfect excuse*. I wasn't really looking for meaningful chat at just this precise moment.

"Now that we have that out of the way," I exited the car and went to the door that opened to my house, "can we go before you end up sleeping in my car?"

Jeremy finally got moving. He followed me inside and up the stairs. When he entered my room, he whistled appreciatively.

"Are those titanium?" he tapped the shutters that sealed my windows.

"Yep, not a sliver of sunlight will get through. And in case a bunch of angry villagers show up with torches and pitchforks, this is also my safe room."

I turned around and gave Jeremy an appraising look. Now in most cases, there would be some sloppy kissing and we could fumble at each other's clothing. I already knew that there would be no kissing. Nothing else would be a greater mood killer than me hurling all over him. I needed to get the motor running somehow, and then inspiration struck.

I pulled my tee shirt off, unclasped my bra and slid out of my pants. All that remained were my blue cotton bikinis. I figured that I could leave a little something for him to deal with. After all, I didn't want to seem easy.

Jeremy unbuttoned his shirt and let it fall. I was extremely pleased with the view. I could see that he worked on his body. Only, did vampires need to do that sort of thing? I mean, they already had the whole superhuman strength thing going on. Did they need to pump iron?

"Are you gonna stare and let your mind wander on whatever little sidetrack that it has started down, or are we going to do this?" Jeremy laughed.

"Sorry," I apologized. I might have blushed if I was able. "I was just admiring your chest and wondering if vampires needed to work out."

"First off, thank you," Jeremy said as he took my hand and pulled me to the bed. "And second...yes. We do need to work out, otherwise we simply start to look like a Ken doll. There is no definition, just a smooth body."

I ran my fingers through the soft, dark brown hair of his chest. I don't get the whole shaved chest thing. I know that some of you ladies like your men to be smooth, but to me it is just creepy. I didn't find twelve-year-old boys attractive when I was twelve years old. Why would I want some guy with a chest smoother than mine?

The only awkward moment was when we each kept trying to kiss each other as things started heating up. Since we both knew how that would end, we managed to veer away, which, admittedly took a little wind out of the sails, but then we both agreed on the good old doggie-style position and our lips could not have met if we'd wanted them to.

Oh don't get all Puritanical on me. What did you think was about to happen? For crying out loud, I've only been saying how horny I was for about the last several pages. Haven't you been paying attention?

But, on the positive side, I have no intentions of trying to give any details. Seriously, that is just not my thing. Besides, then I would have to decide on clever metaphors like "love tunnel" and "velvet cave" or some other equally ridiculous word or phrase to describe my mommy bits down below. And since I am gray, I could hardly refer to my breasts as fleshy mounds. I mean, technically they are still made of flesh, but they are gray! They don't look fleshy so much as stony. I could probably go downtown and stand naked in the Pioneer Square; folks would think I am a statue or something.

I don't know about you, but I get confused when I am sharing sex details. Granted, if it is a friend—like Lisa—I might get all raunchy and put in way too much detail. But here, where you and I don't exactly know each other all that well, I wouldn't know whether I should call his daddy part a penis or a dick…or the more porno-centric term, cock. See, some of you are wincing. At least I am not alone in my discomfort.

What you need to know is this. We did it. We did not kiss. It was okay, but not great. He lasted longer than above average, but since we didn't get too much time to prime my pump, I did not reach the Promised Land. It was still nice, but nothing amazing. Then, apparently the sun came up, because, true to his word, Jeremy died. It was super weird. We were actually talking and he was telling me that we could continue the conversation later. Like a dork, I asked why. Then he just went limp. I mean entirely.

So here is my dirty confession. I already told you that I didn't reach the Grand Finale, so I did something that I am not entirely proud of. I tried to see if he was 'entirely' dead. Are you following me here? In other words, I tried to raise the flag by hand. I figured that there would be no harm if I could get the puppy to sit up. I would hop on, ride to victory, and then go to sleep.

Apparently dead is dead. Now that I think about it, I am a little embarrassed. I probably should have just reached in the drawer beside my bed and handled my own business. Maybe it had something to do with being desensitized to dead bodies. After all, they did make up the basis of my diet.

I recalled that very first corpse that I'd eaten. I was so mortified at the time.

But now for the real revelation. I think this might upset Belinda if she ever finds out what I am about to reveal. Since I find it unlikely that she will ever stoop so low as to read anything that I write…even if it becomes super popular and some cable company decides to make it into a series starring Zooey Deschanel as me. You know how repulsive I have told you that vampires are to my senses? How they absolutely reek? Well, when they are in their dead state…the Dumpster frosting scent goes away. Jeremy smelled so sweet that he made me break out in sharkmouth!

Imagine my surprise when his body shut down and all of a sudden it was as if I were at the peak of my PMS and standing in the middle of a giant fudge factory. I actually drooled on him a bit. I even gave him an experimental lick and he was delish!

Once I got myself under control, I climbed out of bed and into my shower. I had a special set of shower heads installed.

One of them aims in just the right direction. Plus, it has like a dozen settings that pulse at varying degrees of intensity and speeds. I hit the highest settings and rode the waves until my hot water heater finally exhausted itself.

The rest of the day I just watched some daytime television. It made me feel sort of nostalgic. When I was younger and in school, I used to love Spring Break. Not because I went anyplace and flashed my boobs or anything like that. Actually, for me, the best part was just staying in bed late and then watching the soaps while my mom was at work. I've tried a few times in my life to check them out again, but they are just so boring now. I guess we see so much drama in our real lives that the over-the-top stuff they try for now just seems so phony. That, and every actor and actress looks the same.

When my phone rang just after noon, I had a weird feeling. Something told me it was something bad. I've never been much for believing in things like intuition…but then again, I hadn't believed in vampires, zombies, or ghouls.

"Is this Ava Birch?" the strangely familiar voice asked.

"Well since you called me, I imagine that you already know the answer to that question." I always made it a point to give a hard time to telemarketers. And another thing, if I answer my phone and a recording tells me to hold on for "a representative who will get to you shortly," you can bet I hang up. I could care less if I owe you money, or what bill you are trying to collect, but if *you* call me and put *me* on hold…you better believe that I won't be there when you get around to actually being on the phone.

"Hello?" an irritated voice buzzed in my ear.

"Sorry." I really think I might have a problem when it comes to concentration.

"My name is Betty LaGuardia," the voice said. It sounded strangely familiar. "I am calling on behalf of Alessa—"

There was a muffled sound. It sounded like somebody put their hand over the receiver or something. I could make out what sounded like a bit of an argument. After a few moments, the voice returned.

"I am calling on behalf of *Adrianna*," Betty said that name with a hell of a lot of sarcasm.

It struck me. I knew who it was that I was on the phone with; it was that old lady from the porch of that house in Estacada. I had no idea why she would have my number. Even more, I was clueless as to why she would be calling me.

"...says that she wants to meet you face-to-face tonight," Betty said.

"On what terms?" I asked. For some reason, it seemed like I should not be going into this willy-nilly like I did everything else.

I heard Betty repeat my question with her hand not quite covering the receiver of her phone. There was a long silence, and then the sounds of what had to be Adrianna...or Alessa according to Betty's apparent goof, could be made out. I could hear some really angry sounding chatter coming from that end of the line. That was actually a bit of a comfort. Adrianna did not expect me to question things. She really did think that she was dealing with an idiot. When it came to this whole supernatural thing, maybe I wasn't the sharpest knife in the drawer, but I was good on my feet. I had always had the knack of figuring things out on the fly. Granted, it was usually associated to the customer service industry...

"She will offer a truce that will expire in twenty-four hours," Betty related.

That seemed reasonable. I agreed and said that I would be on my way as soon as the sun set.

"And come alone!" I heard a strangely garbled voice hiss in the background.

12

Rosanna

"...absolutely not going out there alone!" Jeremy snarled. He was far too angry for this to just be about my going out to meet Adrianna. I think somebody was compensating for last night/this morning.

"You are not the boss of me," I said as I did an inventory of what I'd put in my bag. I still had absolutely no luck in finding anything that told me how to put a stop to this Queen of the Zombies.

"It isn't about me being the boss of you," Jeremy defended. "But my boss told me that I was not to let you out of my sight. I am supposed to be by your side until she says otherwise."

"And that is really sweet." I patted him on the cheek.

"Don't patronize me, Ava," Jeremy snapped, swatting my hand away. "This is not an order that I can ignore. If you don't allow me to ride with you, I will simply follow you my own way. Estacada isn't that big, you won't be that hard to find."

"Do what you need to do."

Actually, that wasn't such a bad idea. I absolutely did not trust Adrianna. If Jeremy just happened to be in the area and something went wrong, I could hardly be blamed. My only concern was that if this was another one of those damn *ju-ju* thingies, I might suffer from breaking the deal. But if I didn't let him come with me, then technically I was not doing anything

117

wrong.

"About last night..." Jeremy fumbled. Ah-ha, now I was convinced what this whole thing was really about.

"Can we deal with that when I get back? I'd really like to get home early enough so that we can enjoy our next romp in the sack a bit more...if that's okay with you."

My statement was greeted by silence. That was a bit unnerving until I turned around and saw him standing there with his mouth hanging open.

"You better close that thing before it draws flies," I quipped.

I guess that was not exactly the right thing to say. Honestly, I wasn't even thinking about how gross he smells when he is awake. I was not trying to make him self-conscious about being a vampire. Honest.

His face took on a hurt look. Seriously, I was so far from thinking about that Dumpster analogy that I did not know what had his panties in a bunch until he spoke.

"I am sorry if I am so unpleasant for you to be around, but there is nothing that I can do about how a vampire smells to a ghoul. Perhaps now would be the time to tell you that vampires cannot reach absolute sexual fulfillment without at least a slight draw of blood. And since you are a ghoul, your blood would be toxic to me."

So we were going to go the anything-you-can-bitch-about-I-can-bitch-louder route. Nice to know he wasn't above being petty.

"Perhaps you should go back to your little Belinda and tell her that I kicked you out."

"You wouldn't dare." Jeremy's eyes grew large. He glared at me when I simply returned his look with a smile.

"I revoke my invitation," I said in my really bad Clint Eastwood impersonation.

Jeremy wailed and screeched, but a moment later he was outside my front door. I had accidentally done that to Belinda once. It had really pissed her off, but I had learned something that day when it came to dealing with vampires.

"Ava, you can't do this!" Jeremy stood in my doorway.

"Actually," I stepped right up to him and did my best to look fierce, "I can." I shut the door on him and returned to my room to make final preparations.

"Ava, let me back in," Jeremy pleaded. I looked out my window. He was floating just outside. What a showoff.

"Go home, Jeremy." I went over and shut the blinds.

"You don't want to go into this alone."

He was right, I didn't. However, I was not very good at being magnanimous, or whatever the heck that is when somebody says something nasty and you forgive them at the drop of a hat. Oh…now I remember what that is called: weak.

I left my room and went down to my garage. I knew that vampires had freakish speed. What I didn't know was for how long they could keep that up, and just exactly how fast they could go.

I started my Corvette and hit the button on the garage door. When it opened, I wasn't surprised to see Jeremy standing in the middle of the driveway—too bad for him. I knew that hitting him with my car wouldn't kill him. I prepared to shift into reverse and stomp on the gas. That was when I realized that, while it may not do much to the stupid vampire, it might very well put a nasty dent in my precious automobile.

"Fine!" I rolled down my window and yelled. "Get in."

Jeremy's smile was so big that he showed serious fang. That was about to change. Stupid vampire. I shot out of my garage like a rocket. When I hit the street, I yanked hard on my steering wheel, shifted and was gone before he knew what had happened.

Once again, that is a perfect example of a guy thinking that they somehow have the market cornered on a certain skill. I may not be Danica, but I can drive as good if not better when compared to the average guy.

I hit the highway just a Stephen Pearcy was belting out *You Think You're Tough*. I sang along and left one very disgruntled vampire behind. From what he had shared about Belinda, I did not envy him.

As I rolled into Estacada, I was actually very proud of how alert I happened to be. I knew better than to trust Adrianna. Still, if we did not have some sort of showdown, then this little problem was not going to go away anytime soon. That would mean that I would not get paid. It would also mean that Morgan would not be hitting me up with any new gigs any time soon.

I was so 'on the lookout' for anything Adrianna-related that I did not notice the young lady that stepped out in front of my car as I approached the crosswalk and stopped for a red light. She walked right past my hood and up to the passenger's side door. In a jiffy, the lock popped and she opened the door.

I hated it when my fingers and toes went switchblade while I was driving. I can't actually wrap my hands around the steering wheel. Not to mention the fact that I worry about slicing up the carpet on my floorboard. Of course there was also the whole thing about a stranger just getting into my car.

I gave her the full effect of my ghoulish glare as I dropped my glasses and fixed my solid black eyes on her. She just looked back at me and blinked really slow. Her unnaturally green eyes had a glow to them that gave away her supernatural nature. My only problem was that I had no idea what she might be.

"The light changed," she said.

Her voice had an accent from someplace in the United Kingdom. I say that because I couldn't begin to tell you if it was English (the fancy kind, not us American types), Scottish, or Irish. Come to think of it, she might be Australian or from New Zealand. They all sound the same to me. And if you are from one of those places, don't get all twisted. Seriously, can you tell if somebody in America is from Texas, Mississippi, Missouri, South Carolina or Georgia? What about Maine or Massachusetts? Yeah, I didn't think so.

I pulled away from the light and got upset in a big hurry. Normally, everybody has a certain smell to them that I can pick up on. Since all I eat is dead things, I can smell the dead *and* the dying. Because of the fact that everybody is dying slowly, one day at a time if you will, everybody gives off some scent.

If you turned me loose in one of those old folks' homes, I would be like that cat that walks the halls and wanders into a room just before the person dies. And what is the deal with that?

Every few months you see a story like that on the news and people act like it is some sort of big deal. Those cats aren't even *real* cats anyways. But that is a story for another time.

The problem currently facing me was this woman sitting in my car. She had that perfect shade of red hair that no bottle can match. Her skin almost glowed it was so white. Or maybe it did glow; anything was possible when dealing with a supernatural. And the most curious thing was that she gave off no detectable smell.

"So you're a ghoul," she finally said. "Haven't seen one of those for a few hundred years."

I shot her a glance, but decided to keep my mouth shut. One thing that I learned from Morgan is that if you just remain silent, a lot of times the person you are with will run off at the mouth and give you information that you never even thought about trying to find out. Of course I was usually the one doing the talking while Morgan stood there quietly, but at least I was showing the capacity to learn.

"Don't your type usually hang out around graveyards?" this woman asked. She was being totally serious. I just shot her a dirty look and kept driving.

"Of course I imagine things have probably changed over the years. These days, they pump more chemicals in a dead body than you find in your average Twinkie. Probably can't be too tasty. Or is that like junk food for ghouls?"

She sure asked a lot of questions. And she talked really fast. She had one of those squeaky voices that reminded me of Sniffles the mouse from the old cartoons. It didn't actually fit this person. If I was a guy, I'd be sporting serious wood. As it was, I was feeling this strange and unnatural attraction to her that had me a bit uncomfortable. Yes, I've kissed a girl, made out with a couple in my younger experimental days. I just couldn't 'do the deed' if you follow. Right now, I was not so sure that I cared. In case you are the type who needs things spelled out for you…I would munch the carpet, shuck the oyster, tongue the clam. This gal was supernaturally hot.

"Ghouls *can* talk…right?" she pressed. "I mean I know that

you can display this massive mouth with rows of sharp teeth, but you seem to look normal at the moment minus the gray skin and the wicked finger and toenails."

"Yes, I can talk," I finally blurted. However, I was not going to play whatever game this chick had in mind. I also took this moment to slam on the brakes. Obviously she was not going to say anything meaningful…or maybe she would, but I just didn't have the patience. "And just who the blazes are you?"

"My name is Rosanna," she answered. "I'm the one who called Morgan about the zombie that I saw out wandering the woods. Since then, nobody has bothered to call me back. I've spotted three more zombies and had to actually put one down myself. All of them locals, and all of them so old before they were turned that they were practically falling apart beforehand."

"Wait," I said, "you're the witch?"

"I'm *a* witch," Rosanna said with a laugh. "I don't know if I would call myself *the* witch."

"And you say that you have seen three?"

"Including the one tonight? Yes."

"You saw one tonight?"

"Am I going to have to repeat and confirm everything while we talk? Because if that is the case, I can save myself some time and just repeat myself from the get go."

"How about you lose the attitude and just tell me about the zombie that you saw tonight," I urged. I wasn't in the mood to deal with a snarky witch. Actually, I was never in the mood to deal with a snarky anything, but this girl was trying my patience. If she wasn't so hot, I would have kicked her out of the car by now.

"I was at home putting together a few things for some clients…"

Witches had clients? Who knew? I mean, was this a case of her brewing potions and casting spells and stuff for the locals to make people fall in love with each other or what? I wasn't entirely certain what sorts of powers a real witch had. I watched plenty of *Bewitched* when I was younger. I was pretty sure that it wasn't going to be like that. If witches were that powerful, they would control the world. Right?

"…walked right by my window and smashed all of my daisies. If my roses were harmed, I probably would have blown a gasket."

"This was about a flower bed?" I asked in disbelief.

Yes, I can be shallow. Yes, I can often worry about how things might affect me versus how they may impact things on a more global scale. But I have always had that problem. I live in the Pacific Northwest where there are not enough trees for each hugger to get his or her own…and if you have seen the pictures, we have A LOT of trees. This state was sort of the innovator of bottle and can deposits. Everybody…well, *most* everybody is super environmentally conscious. Me, sure, I used the assorted garbage cans. I didn't litter or anything, but I also didn't get all worked up over spotted owls or liquid natural gas pipelines.

Did you know that there were actually people who complained about the windmill farms in the central and eastern part of the state? Yeah, they said they were too noisy and that they scared certain birds or some such nonsense. Yeah, I know. Can't even be happy with so-called 'green' energy. Folks here love to bitch.

"…and I can't brew any for the next several months now thanks to those damn zombies!" Rosanna was almost yelling. Unfortunately, I had probably missed all the important stuff.

"And that probably sucks," I tried to commiserate. "But I think a zombie apocalypse would be much worse than whatever your little problem might be."

"Zombie apocalypse!" Rosanna scoffed. "You have been watching too many movies!"

"Well then, why don't you fill me in if you're so smart."

"For one, Alessa—or whatever she is calling herself these days—can't keep her zombies from falling apart. The ones that I have seen are deteriorating so fast that I doubt they could last long enough to bite somebody. And if they are that weak, then I doubt that they could even pass on the spell."

"Spell?" I asked. "Don't you mean the infection?" I wanted to ask about this other name I kept hearing, but my brain gets too cluttered. I needed to focus on the bits I felt were important.

"Again with too much of the movies or comic books or whatever your source is. Zombies are a magical creature. They have to be imbued with a very powerful spell if they are going to be the type of zombie to create other zombies. Seriously, how could something like just a bite or scratch turn a person into a zombie? It's magic…it certainly is not something seriously scary like AIDS."

Now I was probably more confused than I had been before I met her. Rosanna was saying a whole bunch of stuff, but my mind was not wrapping around the big picture. It was at moments like this that I really missed Lisa.

"But if she is the real reason for the Black Plague, how did it become so wide spread if not by the bite?"

"Oh, the bite has something to do with it, but there is more to it than just being bitten," Rosanna explained. "When a zombie is created to spread its condition to the living, they can only do so within limits. After a dozen or so, they expire and either collapse or just wander aimlessly."

"Like they run out of gas or something?"

"In a way…yes. That is why when you read about the plague, it says that all those people died. That part is correct, but The Queen of the Zombies had to make a few zombies a day and move before being discovered. Then she would make more. The spread had more to do with her being on the run than what the actual zombies did."

"But if she was trying to wipe out the world…" This is the part I really didn't understand. Who would actually want to wipe out the entire world?

"Actually, she was just trying to establish her own kingdom. The problem that she faced is that, unlike tyrannical rulers who might be mean or oppressive, people actually had to be dead to live under the reign of The Queen of the Zombies," Rosanna explained. "They are the perfect…citizen for a lazy ruler. They do what they are told until they are told to stop or do something else. Their most fearsome aspect is that they are a force to be reckoned with on a battlefield."

"So what is her game now? If she knows anything at all, she has to know that nobody here would want to be dead any more than they did in the past."

"I don't think she wants to wipe out the world," Rosanna said with a shrug. "I think that she just wants her own little place where she matters. You see, once she creates a zombie, it is completely devoted to her. It would do whatever she told it to. And she can actually communicate with them and they with her."

"So…what…she is lonely?" That seemed a bit silly. It was certainly no reason to start wiping people out.

"Perhaps," Rosanna said. "She can communicate with the dead in a way that she cannot with the living."

"Like an immigrant worker who doesn't speak good English?" I asked. I realize that probably seems racially insensitive, but it is the best thing that I can come up with, so sue me.

"Perhaps," Rosanna replied. "The bottom line is that she has the need to surround herself with these creatures. They see her not as food or a threat, but rather something to be worshipped. They will obey her to the death."

"Like a dog?" That might have been a better analogy than the whole immigrant worker thing.

"Do you have to ask a thousand questions all the time, or are you just trying to annoy me? It seems like every single time I answer you, you ask me something else…and most of what you are asking is completely irrelevant."

"Listen, witch," somehow this entire conversation had just taken a nasty turn and I had no idea why, "I am new to all this supernatural crap. If you want me to deal with this problem, lose the attitude. Otherwise, if I have a million questions and then a million follow up questions…you just answer them. It is my ass on the line here. As it is, this job has already given me more headaches than I care to deal with."

"What could this have possibly done to impact you?" the witch asked. "I've actually had my gardens stomped flat. I make my living from little brews and potions that I make for a fee. It is my livelihood. Without my garden, I am at the mercy of the council and must offer my services to the regional psychic whenever she sees fit to grace me with a job that is beneath her. Do you have any idea…" Rosanna's voice trailed off as she realized not only what she was saying, but to whom she was saying it.

"I apologize," she whispered. "I meant no disrespect. It is just that I have only been free of Morgan's employment for the past year. I hated feeling like I was something that she—"

"Scraped off her shoe!" I interrupted. "I know, right? It is like, she comes to you with the job and then acts like you are a complete idiot!"

"And she took my familiar a few years ago when I wasn't performing up to her standards and kept her for several months. When I got her back…she was…changed."

"Into a vampire?" I asked, thinking about Lisa and what may have befallen her.

"My cat? Hardly," Rosanna said with a laugh.

"Sorry, just that I have this friend named Lisa who has been with me since right after I turned. She has been like my right hand. I rely on her probably more than a grown woman should considering that Lisa is just a teenager."

"Age has very little to do with a person's mindset," Rosanna said in as serious of a tone as I'd heard from her so far. "When a witch comes into her powers, it is usually around her first bleeding. She is expected to learn how to control her powers within a few months."

"Yes, well I'm still a grown woman who should have a better grasp on things than I do."

"But you say that Morgan has taken this Lisa from you?" Rosanna asked.

"She didn't so much take her as they shared a moment and then there was some whispering. After that, Lisa decided to leave."

"And what sort of creature is Lisa?"

When Rosanna asked that, at first I was taken aback. I mean, what sort of a question was that? Then I remembered that she is a witch and I am a ghoul. It was actually a very good question.

"She is a human."

"A *teen* human?" Rosanna sputtered. "I had no idea that a ghoul could coexist with a human...much less a teenage girl human."

"It's not like I would eat her or something," I huffed. "She is perfectly safe with me."

"Perhaps things have changed over the centuries," Rosanna said with some serious doubt ringing in her voice.

"What is that supposed to mean?"

"It's just that, for as long as I've been aware of their existence, ghouls are more like the assassins of the supernatural world. It is said that there is no more fierce a fighter than a ghoul. They are almost impervious to pain, and possess great power in battle. And in this day and age, their ability to...if you will excuse the blatancy...eat the evidence—"

"Wait a second," I interrupted. "You are saying that my supernatural job description is basically that of a killer?"

"That is one way to look at it. It's just that ghouls were always sought by any who desired to rise to power. They are killing machines. Their ability to ignore pain is the thing of legends. To capture one is pointless because they are immune to torture."

"But what about the sun? I burn like an albino in the desert."

I imagine that most of you are now immune to my lack of political correctness. Seriously, you can't say midget, you can't say black or oriental, and somebody just told me that albino is insensitive. Well that settles it; I am demanding that my publisher post something in the description of this series about my so-called insensitivity. I'll be damned if I am going to tiptoe through the PC crap. I bet most of you don't either unless your more 'worldly' friends are around. C'mon, you know the ones I am talking about, the type who refuses to say "Merry Christmas" and all that.

To quote one of my heroes, Joan Rivers, "Can we talk?" I bet if you are reading this...or even more accurately...*still* reading this book, then you are the kind of person who watches

South Park and wishes you'd have thought to make the same observations about whatever or whoever they are making fun of currently. More accurately, you wish you could say some of it in public without having the locals show up with torches and pitchforks.

I'm not saying that there isn't a line. But most people don't even get close enough to see the line these days. I was with some friends at lunch one day and one of the girls said something was "totally gay." Now from the reaction of one of the other ladies sitting at the table, you would have thought that the "N-word" had been used. (Yes, that is a line I will not cross. The Black community and Eminem can say what they like…but I will take a pass on that one.)

"Ava!" Rosanna yelled.

Damn, I was doing it again, wasn't I?

"Did you hear anything that I just said?"

I gave a sheepish shake of the head. *Bad Ava…that is a very bad Ava.*

"I said that it is a law in the supernatural community. Each of us, for some reason or another has issues with the sun. That is considered the equivalent of the nuclear option. Anybody who might consider using it knows that supernaturals from around the world would hunt them down and kill them. Enemies would set aside their differences to kill whoever would consider using the sun as a weapon."

"Wait, so how are witches bothered by the sun?" I knew for a fact that it burned my skin instantly. I also knew that it was death to a vampire, but what could it possibly do to a witch?

"If we are exposed to the sun for a period of four hours, it erases our power," Rosanna said after a brief pause. I think she was weighing the trust level. She was about to expose a serious weakness. In the end, I imagine that she knew I would find out one way or the other.

"Seems to me like a simple burning at the stake would be much quicker." I really do have that problem of speaking before thinking. I clamped my mouth shut and dared to risk a look at Rosanna. She was smiling! WTF?

"You are obviously referring to the old stories about Salem and the trials."

I nodded. I was a little surprised that she wasn't fuming. I mean, that would be like cracking slavery jokes with the head of the NAACP or Spike Lee.

"Do you think that a human would have stood a chance had they been dealing with any *real* witches?" She had a point. "A real witch would have known what was coming and considering the primitive times that this took place, it would have been nothing for her to wipe out the entire town."

"You always say her...like as in one. What about covens?" I asked. I figured since she was so full of information, and obviously not shy about sharing, I should ask whatever came to mind. You never know when that information will come in handy.

"Covens!" Rosanna laughed. If she would have been drinking something, it would have shot out her nose. "Covens are silly little human constructs. The thing about mortals is that they seek acceptance. Even when they are trying to seem like they are on the fringe and unique, they always tend to surround themselves with likeminded individuals."

"So you witches don't gather and perform rituals while dancing naked under the light of the moon."

"Would you want somebody watching you dance naked?" she asked. "Especially another woman?"

"Good point," I agreed.

"But we have strayed well off the subject of The Queen of the Zombies," Rosanna sighed.

"And apparently out of town," I added.

I looked around and realized that we had driven out into the middle of nowhere. There was nothing but trees and more trees surrounding us.

I turned us around and headed back to town. Rosanna was silent as I drove. I imagine that she was afraid to say anything. For as grouchy as she got about me asking too many questions, she was certainly a fountain of information. That girl could talk. I decided to test something.

"So what did losing your familiar do to you? Did it hurt?"

"I was powerless for almost a month. It is like an illness. And then, once I recovered, I had to summon a new one and then create the bond from scratch."

"But I thought you said the other one came back?"

"I was forced to put her down. She was no longer an open channel for my magic."

13

Rainbow in the Dark

Just as I was re-entering Estacada, a weird "flash" lit up the sky. I put flash in quotes because I doubt it was actually visible to humans. I say this since we were driving past a few when the entire sky turned an ugly purple for about two seconds and then went back to normal and none of them so much as even glanced up.

"Interesting," Rosanna murmured.

Then she pulled this little bag out and started digging through it. I knew it was a special bag when she pulled out a shotgun and a half dozen bottles that I at first thought were wine. You know those bottles that come with the wicker basket woven around the bottom? You usually get them in Italian places. You always take the bottle home and then use it for a candle holder. Now you know the ones I'm talking about, don't you?

"What was that?" Leave it to me to ask the super-obvious question.

"I believe that was a message for you," Rosanna continued to dig through her bag. I almost expected her to climb inside the damn thing.

"It was a message?"

"Somebody is in danger and needs you desperately if I read it correctly."

Now I was really curious. There is not really anybody who

knows me, much less one that would call me for help in any case.

Rosanna pulled out these weird goggles and slipped them on. She stuck her hand out the window and looked up. Then she started whispering a bunch of stuff that I am pretty sure was Latin.

"Oh yeah, it's for you alright."

"Does it say who it is from?"

"No, nothing like that," Rosanna said as she took off her goggles and tossed them back into the bag. "But whoever it is has an urgent need for you to help them right away."

"Where do I go? Does it at least say that?"

"Messages like this only come from graveyards."

"Swell."

Rosanna had to direct me to the graveyard. However, once we were just a few blocks away, she had me stop the car.

"This is where I get out, Ava."

"But what if I need your help?"

She laughed! I didn't see what was so damn funny. I waited for a moment, thinking that once she was done with her laughter, she would respond to my question. Instead, she simply kept laughing as she walked away.

I pulled up to the graveyard and just sat in my car. For some reason, my precious Corvette was not bringing me any comfort. I thumbed through a few songs until I came to the song *Suite Sister Mary*. I may piss a few people off, but those of you who have come to know me will already realize that I don't give a rat's puckered patootie. I think that the *Operation: Mindcrime* album rivals Pink Floyd's *The Wall*. And as far as an in depth story, it isn't even close.

This particular song is one that I used to like to listen to when I was in a funk. For one, Geoff Tate is at his multi-octave register best in this baby. But there is so much passion in this song. If you have no idea what I am talking about, I highly recommend that you seek it out and give it a listen.

Something told me that it was about to get intense and that whoever called was doing so because of Adrianna. My fingers and toes were tingling and I had this new sensation in my head that I could not identify.

For those of you who were wishing that I would have saved us all the trouble and knocked off The Queen of the Zombies way back at Voodoo Doughnut, I was suddenly seeing your point of view. Drama and exciting tension be damned…I was about to go head-to-head with the individual responsible for wiping out about half of the population a few centuries ago. I was way out of my league on this one.

"Ava!" a familiar voice called.

If I would have moved my head much quicker, I might have snapped my own neck. Never in my life have I been simultaneously so happy and so worried in my life.

"Lisa!" I threw open my car door, climbed out, and loped to the huge arched gate that would open to the graveyard if the place were actually open.

I skidded to a stop. Having lived with her for a while, I was very familiar with Lisa's scent. This was Lisa, of that I had no doubt, but she had no scent. I sniffed the air again just to be sure. Nope, not a thing was coming to me from her. That was all it took to finish my fingers and toes.

"Whoa!" Lisa exclaimed, taking a step back. "It's me. Don't get crazy here."

"How come I can't smell you?"

"You can't what?" Lisa sounded confused.

"You know about my sense of smell…or at least *Lisa* knows about it." I was suddenly very wary of the person standing before me. She looked exactly like Lisa, but smell is a sense that many shrinks say create the most lasting images and memories.

For me, a ghoul, smell is huge. I was suddenly struck by the peculiar rituals that all dogs go through when they met each other. You know what I'm talking about. Yeah…that whole butt sniffing thing.

I could be robbed of all my senses as long as I had smell and still function pretty damn good. I could pick Lisa out in a store on Black Friday if that gives you any idea. That's not bragging. I actually had to do that to find her this past day after Thanksgiving. Actually, it was Shameful Thursday. We couldn't wait to shop and went out to a few of the sales that kicked off on Thanksgiving Day at 8PM.

I am embarrassed to say that not only did I go, but if I can save that kind of money on a 70-inch, HD, 3D television…then you poor little retail clones are screwed.

Sure, I saw all the people bitching and moaning about the "poor Walmart workers" and such. If you are working at Walmart, that day on the clock did not come as a surprise. And besides, I saw a great post that shut down a lot of the boo hoo crybabies. It was a guy in full combat gear in some horrific Middle East shit hole. It basically said something like "Walmart employees have to work at 8PM on Thanksgiving?! So." Of course it doesn't really get the justice it deserves when I share it here minus the pictures…and the two hundred-plus post thread where all the people are bitching.

"Same old Ava," Lisa laughed. Or at least the girl that sure looked a lot like Lisa did.

"What?"

"I asked you the same question four times and you just stood there with a blank expression on your face."

Dammit!

"Okay, what was your question?" I shot back.

"I asked if you remembered when Morgan and I whispered a little something just before I left?"

"How could I forget? You just packed up and walked out of our house right after."

"Yes," Lisa agreed. "But I left with a purpose."

I kept my mouth shut. Seriously, the only thing coming to mind was dripping with sarcasm and nastiness. If I said it and this was really Lisa and she was trying to come back to me or whatever, then opening my big mouth was a bad idea.

"Morgan said that I could choose a number of paths that would lessen the amount of danger that I ended up being in when we went out into these crazy situations together. She said that it was obvious that I cared about you a great deal, and that I would eventually get myself killed if I kept it up."

A number of scenarios flashed through my mind. The worst being that she went to Belinda's and became a vampire. I really did not like that idea. I would feel like it was all my fault. Actually, I am pretty sure it is anyways.

"And so what exactly did you do?" I tried to keep a lid on my emotions, but it wasn't working. "And what was it that you could whisper back and forth with Morgan that you felt you needed to keep secret from me?"

When you got down to it, there I was being just plain old selfish Ava. *She* was making some sort of life-changing decision, and I wanted to know why she was keeping secrets from *me*. I could feel guilty about that later; right now I just wanted answers.

"She said that if I was going to remain a part of your life, I needed to take some steps to ensure my own safety. She said that you would never forgive yourself if something happened to me, and that despite the fact that it was my choice and my own free will to stay with you and go on these…adventures…that it was irresponsible of me to remain in danger. She said that if something happened to me, you might very well become a serious danger to yourself and everybody else out of feelings of misery and self-pity."

I couldn't argue with her logic.

"So I was given a few choices that she felt might interest me."

This is where my blood would run cold…if it actually ran. I was curious, but I was also terrified as to what those 'choices' might include.

"Just tell me that you did not become a vampire." For some reason, that was the worst possible choice she could make. Don't ask me why, but my mind was so fixated on that one thing that I could not even fathom that there might be other choices.

"Morgan says that I have some minor psychic talents," Lisa announced.

"So what…you are going to train with her and take over your own territory?" That might be almost as bad. I could not imagine Lisa sporting Morgan's attitude.

"No...I said that I have some *minor* talents. So I could actually train with the Templars."

That statement just seemed to hang in the air. I know that seems a bit cliché, but I was struck dumb. I had nothing to say. Probably the biggest reason had to do with the fact that I had not ever actually met a Templar. I didn't really know what they did. I did seem to recall that they never give the impression that they are on the side of good in any of the movies. But what did movies know? How many ghouls can you name that are not mindless monsters?

"And what would that mean? How would that keep you safe?" I asked what I considered to be the most obvious question.

"The Templars are trained defenders. They learn all the latest combat techniques."

"So you would be like some sort of bad ass...like Uma Thurman in *Kill Bill*?"

"Yeah, but even better. I would learn all this really cool hand-to-hand combat stuff."

"That still doesn't explain why you have no scent. Unless you—"

"I already met with the Guardian of the West," Lisa blurted. "He talked with me for a while and then had me do a few tests. Things like stand still for hours and then some freaky stuff with a series of pretty gross pictures where I was supposed to look and then a few hours later I had recite everything that I remembered about a particular scene. I guess I did okay, because I have been invited to attend the first stage of training. If I pass I can continue and eventually become an actual Templar. But I had to accept the Initiate's Ring."

She flashed her hand and I saw what looked like nothing more than a regular old white gold band. You know the type that people buy when they want to get married and can't afford much beyond next month's rent.

"And am I correct to assume that this ring has some sort of magic property?"

"It halts my aging process. If I remain a Templar, I will

eventually receive a much nicer ring that looks fancy, but really just does the same thing as this one."

"So then why did you feel the need to send me up a distress signal? You don't think that this is something that we could talk about at home?"

"But I didn't send you any distress signal."

Almost on cue, a scream pierced the air from somewhere deeper inside the cemetery. The only thing that I could tell for certain was that it was a female.

"I should probably check on that." I tried my best to walk towards the entry gate—which also meant walking past Lisa—without looking like I was bothered. After all, she was talking about taking on something that had nothing to do with me. I guess I always expected her to simply be my sidekick. I guess that was the problem. If she was going to stay with me, then her mortality was her biggest liability.

As I passed her, Lisa took my hand. Even though my fingernails were on full alert, she didn't even flinch. And then I noticed...she didn't flinch! Lisa always had a problem with touching me. Do I need to remind you that when you touch a real person, they are warm? My skin was cool to the touch. After all, I am a ghoul.

"I'll come with you," she said with a smile.

"So you take a few tests and get a ring, and now you are some sort of ass-kicking super hero?"

"Nope, but you have kept me safe so far. Unless something has changed, I should be fine."

Another one of those odd flashes lit up the sky. This one was almost blinding. I must have ducked instinctively.

"Are you okay, Ava?" Lisa asked.

"You didn't see that?"

"See what?"

"That crazy flash that just lit up the entire sky with ugly swirls of purple!"

"Sorry, I didn't see a thing."

"Well then, if you are coming with me, grab my bag from the car and let's go see what this is all about."

"Something tells me that I could eventually be the Grand Templar and I will still be carrying your bag," Lisa grumbled.

Glad to see that some things hadn't changed.

11

Unchained

We were weaving through the stones when another scream came. This one was much weaker. The only good thing about it was that it gave us a better direction.

So let me ask a question. Why do they always want to build graveyards on hills and slopes? Don't they know that monsters and evil villains always hide on the other side of those things?

We reached the top of the tree-dotted mound and found the source of the distress call that had brought me here. Laid out on one of the big tombs was a young girl. Only, it was already very clear that she was no ordinary human girl. The big give away? Her eyes were glowing a bright blue.

Standing over her was Adrianna. Only, she was in full 'Queen of the Zombies' mode. Her skin had gone all mottled and gray, her eyes were a jaundiced yellow. And that really fashionable hairstyle? Oh yeah…gone. Her hair was a tangled mop of filth. I was pretty sure stuff was moving in it.

She was wearing what looked like little more than a burlap sack. It was tattered and dirty with rips and holes revealing more skin than she probably should in this form. Her arms were entirely bare and you could see sores that oozed pus *and* maggots! I know, as if either one were not bad all by itself, she had both going on at once from the same sores.

And then the smell hit me. The next thing that I know, I am

on my back looking at the sky. Seriously, how does something smell so good that it causes an orgasm? Only, it wasn't a sexual orgasm in my hoo-hoo area. This was a full body experience.

On the plus side, I now had sharkmouth along with my switchblade fingers and toes. Lisa's face was over mine and she was saying something, but I couldn't really hear anything. All I could see, hear, or smell was coming from Adrianna.

"Ava, look at me!" Lisa yelled as she slapped me in the face.

Can I ask a question? What in the hell is that supposed to accomplish. You see it in the movies all the time. Somebody is out of it, or even worse, hysterical. The person with them always has to slap them in the face. Seriously, all that did was piss me off. Hmm...maybe *that* was the point.

"Mrgglph!" Yeah, I can't say much when I am rocking the sharkmouth, but if I would have been able to speak, it would have had something to do with letting Lisa know that if she hit me again, she might become the first one-handed Templar.

"So nice of you to join us," Adrianna chortled.

For those of you who don't know, a chortle is kind of like that laugh you heard from that big Wookie in the *Star Wars* movies. It is a deep and odd sounding laugh. At least that is what I am using to categorize them.

"Looks like you're a little busy," Lisa said after giving me a look and seeing that the sharkmouth wasn't going to go away this very minute.

"And what do we have here?" Adrianna stepped around the tall, flat grave stone that she had bound this mysterious creature to and folded her scabby arms under her oddly still firm breasts. I've said it before, but it bears repeating...life is so not fair.

"I was the one sitting out in the car," Lisa answered. "The one you wanted to use in some sort of twisted ritual."

"Ah yes, the little slut who can't keep her legs together like a proper lady," Adrianna sniffed. "What is it with your generation? Did you know that there is an entire program on the television dedicated to sixteen-year-old whores who become impregnated? Your society as a whole could use some cleansing.

You are a particularly nasty bunch."

Ouch. Seriously, she did have a point. Not that I believed society as a whole needed to be wiped out. Just a select few…like the reality show whores. Oh yeah, and a few of those folks on that show *Cheaters*…and maybe the guy who hosts that program. Also people who get in line at the grocery store express lane with a full shopping cart, a folder full of coupons, and a checkbook.

"…how hard it was to find a virgin who met the qualifications required for me to cast my spell?" Adrianna was still ranting.

"But that isn't just a girl," Lisa pointed to whatever that thing was that continued to squirm against the bonds keeping her tied to the marble slab.

"And I can't wait to find out just how much more powerful my spell will be," Adrianna cackled.

Now, for those of you wondering what might be the difference between a cackle and a chortle, a cackle is like what that witch on *Wizard of Oz* did all the time. So if you think I am just randomly selecting synonyms for the word 'laugh' then you would be mistaken.

"I won't let you get away with this," I said, stepping past Lisa.

Wait! Where did sharkmouth go? Lisa looked just as surprised as me. I gave her my usual 'how the heck should I know' shrug and started down the little mound to where Adrianna was standing. She had a funny look on her face, and I would be willing to bet that she was just as surprised as Lisa and I about this new development.

"Interesting," was all Adrianna muttered. She raised a dagger above her head and shouted something. Again, I was pretty sure that it was Latin.

"Don't do it, Adrianna," I growled as I started towards her.

So here is a question. Why is it that all of these damn weirdoes need to sacrifice naked girls? And what is the deal with always having to cut them up with an ornamental dagger? It just seems a bit tired. Think of how many times you have seen this particular moment in a "horror" movie.

In just a couple of steps, I was on the other side of the slab. I glanced down at the girl. She was crying, but her tears were all sparkly. I had to actually pull myself away from her eyes. In their bizarre blue glow I could almost swear that those tears were turning into diamonds...but that was just silly. It had to be all the magic or whatever was in the air.

"Time for you to go to sleep, Ava," Adrianna whispered.

"Ghouls don't sleep," I shot back.

Something in my mind was feeling all wiggly. I truly felt something move in my head! That is just too creepy. I don't know if you have ever had a serious intestinal virus. You know the kind where you can actually feel things move through your system? It is icky and uncomfortable, I won't get into the particulars, but I think you know what I mean.

"...shouldn't be able to resist that!" Adrianna hissed.

Uh-oh, I was doing it again. Obviously Adrianna was not happy. That much was certain. I gave her a close look. Now that I was standing right here in front of her, I could see her skin. It looked like parchment paper. In fact, bits of it were peeling up in places along her bare arms wherever there was not one of those open sores all crawling with maggots.

One particular piece of her arm was all peeled back and a flap of dry skin sort of waved in the night breeze. I couldn't help myself. I reached over and plucked it like a potato chip.

"What are you doing?" The Queen of the Zombies screamed. I couldn't tell if it was anger or frustration, but she was being super emotional. "I command you to stop! Return to where you came and forget!"

I popped that little flake of skin in my mouth. It was so good. When I was a little girl, I went to Catholic school for two years—seventh and eighth grade. I still have the uniforms...well, not the same ones from back then, but I dated this one guy. Sorry, that is a story for another time. Anyways, one of the stories I always enjoyed was that whole Moses thing. I still like to watch *The Ten Commandments* every Easter. But when they get the manna, that bread from Heaven, and the description is that it was sweeter than honey and completely fulfilling; that was like this little piece of dried arm skin that I plucked from Adrianna and ate.

"...as I command you!" Now Adrianna was screaming. In fact, the girl on the slab had gone quiet and was watching The Queen of the Zombies.

"Command me?" I laughed. "I'm not one of your zombies. You don't command anything here, sister."

"Ava?" Lisa called. Something about her voice was peculiar.

"What?" I didn't want to take my eyes off of Adrianna, so I just hollered over my shoulder.

"How are you doing that?" she asked.

"Doing what?"

"You can't ever talk through the sharkmouth."

I reached up and touched my face. Sure enough, I could feel the wide rows of razors that made up a grill that would rival a great white shark. But if that was the case, then how *was* I talking? Lisa hadn't been looking at me weird because I had shrugged it off; she was looking at me because I was talking with sharkmouth in effect.

"This can't be happening," Adrianna insisted.

"I know," I agreed. "This is freaky." I wished at that moment that I had a mirror. I wondered what it looked like when I talked with my sharkmouth. I bet it was cartoonish...something from a Pixar film.

"Not your mouth, you idiot!" Adrianna spat.

"So we are going to be rude?" I asked, and then my eyes fixed on another strip of dried skin dangling from her chin. Before she could react to my gaze, I reached over and snatched it. If possible, it was even tastier than the first piece.

"You are yummy."

I actually felt a huge gob of slobber roll down my chin. I didn't care. If those little strips were that good, I bet she would be the equivalent of Thanksgiving and every flavor of Ben & Jerry's all at once. And I mean that in a good way. Not like ice cream on turkey or something freaky. I am just talking about the satisfaction aspect.

"I wonder what a whole arm would taste like," I gurgled as I fixated on another piece of skin dangling near the elbow.

"Ava?" Lisa was beside me now. I gave her a look and she actually winced. "Your eyes."

"What about them?" I asked, those very eyes unable to look away from that delectable morsel that was just hanging there waiting for me to pluck it like a grape.

"They are swirling," Lisa said. She was actually leaning forward over that poor girl that was still tied to the slab.

"Like the hypno-toad?" I giggled.

"Huh?"

"Nothing," I said with a dismissive wave. Less talking, Ava want yummy treat.

"I am serious, Ava," Lisa insisted. Something in her voice was trying to chisel into my brain. "Your eyes are doing something that I've never seen. They look like—"

"Galaxies," Adrianna and the girl on the table both spoke.

"Stop changing the subject!" I said. That was when I heard it. My voice was different!

When Adrianna is in her full Queen of the Zombies glory—like right now—she has this thing that happens to her voice that sounds like two people talking at once. One is just her regular voice, but the other is really deep and kind of makes your innards quiver. They are on top of each other. It sounds creepy, but it is totally something that you would expect from somebody who calls herself The Queen of the Zombies. And did I ever mention that, when she refers to herself in the third person using that title, you can actually hear the word 'the' capitalized? Seriously.

"…perhaps you would agree to that." Adrianna had been talking again. Oops.

"That's it!" Lisa smacked me.

"Ow!" I rubbed my arm. It didn't actually hurt, but it sounded like it should.

You ever do that? Something happens and you just habitually say 'ouch' or make a noise. Then you are sort of committed to acting like something hurt that really didn't?

"Compartmentalizing," Adrianna sighed. "I had heard that ghouls were capable, but only the more powerful ones. I certainly did not expect this from *you*."

"Hey!" She didn't have to be nasty about it.

"So what are you going to do with her?" Lisa asked, nodding to Adrianna. She didn't even bother to ask, she just started to unbuckle the wrist cuffs that held the girl-shaped thing lying naked on the slab.

"She is really yummy," I said around my fully functional sharkmouth.

"Can you stop thinking with your stomach long enough to let me propose a deal?" Adrianna threw her hands up.

I was actually really disappointed. This all seemed so anticlimactic. I bet you were expecting some long fight scene, weren't you? Well not everything has to end in violence. Maybe you should evaluate your own self for a moment. Does every conflict in your life have to end in a fight? No? Well why should it in mine?

"...your authority," Adrianna said. She raised her eyebrows in question.

"If you surrender to her then you have to allow Morgan to inspect your containment to ensure that there is no way for you to escape," Lisa said after giving me an elbow in the ribs.

"That ring!" Adrianna's tone changed in an instant.

She backed up a few steps. As things had begun winding down, she started returning to her human-looking likeness...the pretty one without all the yummy skin flaps and maggot-filled sores. Right now she was pointing at Lisa like the girl was a poisonous snake.

"This little thing?" Lisa flashed her Templar secret decoder ring or whatever she wanted to call it. Adrianna winced and took another few steps back.

"How is a Templar in league with a ghoul?"

I looked at Lisa and we both shrugged. I returned my attention to Adrianna. She was caught in this sickly in-between transformation that was in reality quite hideous. Still perfectly firm and perky breasts…bitch.

"The Templars practically wiped out all the ghouls centuries ago. That is why I was so surprised to meet you and discover what you were." Adrianna now seemed way more worried about Lisa than she did about me. "To see one working *with* a ghoul is unheard of."

"I have no idea what you are talking about," Lisa said. "And I really haven't been involved with the Templars for very long."

"This just keeps getting better," Adrianna muttered.

"Thank you, miss," the girl gasped and rolled off the table after Lisa unbuckled the final restraint.

"Not a problem," Lisa said, reaching to help the girl steady herself on her feet.

"Not you," she said in a surprisingly nasty tone as she backed away from Lisa and wiped at her skin like it might be contaminated or crawling with bugs. "I meant *you*."

I had to look over my shoulder. I seriously did not think that she could be talking to me. After all, I hadn't really done all that much…except take a few nibbles on The Queen of the Zombies and discover that I could talk around my sharkmouth. My head was suddenly spinning with all that had just taken place. It was pretty amazing for a Thursday night.

"Uh…you're welcome?" I wasn't sure what this was all about. Then I realized that I still did not have a clue as to what this 'girl' might be. "And just for my own curiosity, what manner of supernatural are you?"

"A siren, miss," the girl said.

Now, here is the scene. It is the middle of the night. I am standing with a wanna-be Templar, The Queen of the Zombies, and now apparently a siren—whatever those are—who is as naked as the day that God put her on this earth. And she does not seem bothered even just a teensy bit about the whole standing-naked-in-front-of-strangers thing.

Of course, she has perfect skin, amazing red hair, another damn set of perfect little boobies…and lookie here….somebody likes to keep the playground free of grass if you know what I mean. And then there is that cute little accent. I was going to step out on a limb and guess Irish.

"Okay, fill in the stupid ghoul...what is a siren?" I had to ask.

"We sing on the waters, miss," the girl said like that explained everything. Fine, I could look it up later.

I have so much crap to learn. I think I am going to go to a hobby store and by one of those silly *Dungeons & Dragons* books. I bet at least that way I would have a list of monsters to start looking up.

"Ava!" a voice called, sounding frantic.

Seems that I had forgotten all about Jeremy in the fuss. He was walking across the graveyard with a very cranky look on his face. Then he reached the group and froze.

"Is that a..." his voice trailed off as he stared first at Lisa, and then at Adrianna, and finally the siren. Which reminded me...

"Hey?" I touched the siren girl on her arm. "I don't even know your name."

"It is Aoife, miss."

"Eye-fa?" What kind of name is that?"

"Gaelic, miss."

"And stop calling me 'miss', my name is Ava."

"Yes, m—" she paused. "Yes, Ava."

"Now, one thing at a time. Jeremy, I told you I didn't need your help. So go home...or wherever it is you sleep. Lisa, we can talk about what the Templars may or not have up their little sleeves later...alone. And after I have words with Morgan. Aoife, you are free to go, but I have a question, was that you who made the sky do that flash thing?"

"No." She looked confused as to what I was talking about. So if it wasn't Lisa, and it wasn't Aoife, that left—

"It was me," an old woman said as she stepped out of the shadows.

"Betty?" Boy was I confused.

"You know my name?" the old woman asked as she walked up beside Adrianna, casting a very nasty look her way.

"Well, you did call me that one time, plus, I was sort of

eavesdropping outside of your house the other night," I admitted.

"Then you know what this little whelp did to my Horace?"

"If you mean the whole turn him into a zombie thing? Yeah, I know about that."

"Well I demand to have a say in the dealings with this one." She cocked her head towards Adrianna. There was something about this old woman that oozed power. I have no idea why I hadn't picked up on it earlier.

"Nothing has been decided yet," I said with a shrug. "What do you have in mind?"

As Betty began to speak, there were a few gasps and one very pathetic moan from The Queen of the Zombies. Lisa's jaw dropped once or twice and Aoife was oddly silent, showing absolutely no emotion. She did however continue to simply stand there naked like it was no big deal. And you can bet that I noticed each and every lingering glance that Jeremy shot her way.

When it was all over, I at least had a plan. I didn't think that Morgan was going to like it, but she was in no position to complain. I'd discovered a few things in the past few hours that changed the dynamics of our relationship.

15

Lack of Communication

"And who do you think you are, making demands and conditions to *me!*" Morgan was about to bust a gasket.

"How about you answer my question?" I was trying hard to control my anger. I could feel my fingers and toes starting to tingle.

"Yes, I suggested that she speak with the representative from the Templars. They excel at defense and if that child is going to continue to tag along despite my warnings, and if you don't have the ability to make her stay home when she has no business being with you, then it is my belief that she could use some help. Help that you could not provide."

"And so you sent her to the folks who tried to completely wipe out every ghoul in existence," I growled, stepping way inside Morgan's personal space. It was a statement, not a question. And after speaking with Betty, I had a few other tricks up my sleeve, but I could save them for later.

"That was half a millennium ago!" Morgan's voice had gotten just a touch louder.

Considering the fact that she had shown almost zero emotion in all of our dealings, this was the equivalent of a nuclear event. So far, she had sputtered twice, stammered once, raised her voice, and the cherry on the sundae—a scowl.

"I am supposed to be extinct," I said. I could feel

sharkmouth coming. Now it was time to see if I had actually learned anything last night. I looked at Morgan and tried to let my mind wander.

"History is full of mistakes made by groups who thought that they were operating in the best interests of society. What would it be like if everybody still equated this country with its use of slaves?"

I remembered sitting on my living room floor when I was little. Everybody was all excited about this mini-series called *Roots*. I tried so hard to watch it, but I was only in third or fourth grade. I never stayed awake for a whole episode...

"We are talking about genocide." I was really proud that I had remembered the word Betty used. The problem now was that I couldn't tell if the look on Morgan's face was from my use of that word or from something else. I very casually went to tuck my hair behind my ear. I felt this odd leathery stuff where my cheek was supposed to be, and then I brushed one of the jagged teeth. Yay!

"W-w-what are you doing?" Morgan actually looked to turn just a touch paler. That was a stretch considering how she was already the color of bleached ivory.

"I am asking you a question," I said, trying my best not to smile. I've seen my smile with sharkmouth going, and it is not something that puts me in my most flattering light.

"Don't play games with me, Ava Birch." Morgan stood straight and seemed to draw all of the emotion that she'd just been displaying back into her body and erase any evidence of its prior existence.

"You have been keeping me in the dark, Morgan. I have been learning all sorts of interesting things the past day or two. So, the way I see it, you need me. In fact, having me in your district is quite a little victory for a psychic. From what I hear, I am worth more to you than you have been letting on. And since I now know a few things like what happened to Solomon's treasure and the vast wealth once kept in vaults under the Vatican, I also know that you can afford to pay me better and supply me with things when I go on these little clean-up missions for you."

Morgan didn't say a word; she just stood there glaring at me. Funny thing is that just about forty-eight hours ago something like that would have mattered. Unfortunately for her, I had discovered a few things. It is not unlike being the lone brain surgeon in a hospital…I have a special skill that very few possess— as well as some that I don't think that I have discovered yet. After all, until last night I didn't think that I could talk with the sharkmouth in effect.

Also, according to Betty, I have the ability to compartmentalize my mind. She said I am like a computer in that I can actually do multiple things in my head at once. That is what makes a ghoul so dangerous. Apparently we can overcome just about any type of magic.

A ghoul has a few things that happen automatically—kind of like a store-bought computer with a bunch of software. That is why vampires have no effect on me with their gaze or mind control. Our fingers and toes becoming weapons, and the sharkmouth. However, there is apparently a great deal to learn.

I also discovered that Morgan actually can read minds to a certain extent. However, a ghoul is like white noise. Part of what makes us so valuable is that we can operate independently and actually put the regional psychic in check should the need arise. Apparently there is a council of psychics, and Morgan having me in her region makes her a bit more powerful, because I can actually enter another district undetected. It was a group of psychics that apparently hired the Templars to wipe us out.

That brought to mind a few questions. Was she keeping tabs on me through Lisa? Also, what better way to keep tabs on the Templars than to have somebody close, and then later she could poke around in her brain? That Morgan is a slippery one. I will have to keep on my toes. And who knew that the supernatural community had so much drama attached to it? It is all about power plays and one-upsmanship.

So, a few words about Betty. It seems that she is related through blood to Adrianna. She does not delve in zombies, though. She is a little hazy on her actual background, but I think she is pretty damn powerful. The way that she shut Adrianna down in the graveyard, plus the things that she did actually tell me—more than Morgan has in all the time I've known her—leads me to believe that she would be a good person to have as an ally. For now I am keeping her my own little secret.

But, Ava, you might be asking yourself, if Morgan can read Lisa's mind, what is to keep her from finding things out that way? For one, that little memory wipe ability that The Queen of the Zombies used on me…apparently it is a family secret. Lisa doesn't remember a thing about Betty. Even better, I could tell her all about Betty right now and it would be like pouring water through a sieve. It would just fall right back out. Pretty cool, huh?

"Enjoy this moment for now, Ava," Morgan was standing in the doorway. Obviously she was leaving. That made me wonder what I had just missed because Lisa looked just a little pale…like something had her spooked.

"Don't threaten me anymore, Morgan," I said as I stepped to the door and prepared to shut it. "I know more about my worth now…you better come with a new tactic when you are dealing with me."

And then I shut the door. I was not going to let her have the last word. I turned to say something to Lisa about how freaking awesome it was to have the last word for a change, but she was gone. I homed in on her and discovered that she had gone to her room.

Oh well…I don't need an audience. I feel pretty damn good about things. I just wish that Betty had given me a few more words of advice and instruction. I wasn't terribly fond of having Adrianna confined in my basement.

<u>Other Titles by TW Brown</u>

The DEAD Series:

DEAD: The Ugly Beginning
DEAD: Revelations
DEAD: Fortunes & Failures
DEAD: Winter
DEAD: Siege & Survival

DEAD Special Edition

DEAD: Steve's Story
DEAD: Vignettes
DEAD: The Geeks
DEAD: Compendium 1

Zomblog

Zomblog
Zomblog II
Zomblog: The Final Entry
Zomblog: Compendium
Zomblog: Snoe

Miscellaneous

Gruesomely Grimm Zombie Tales Vol. I
That Ghoul Ava
Dakota (as Todd Brown)

**The growing voice in horror
and speculative fiction.**

Find us at www.maydecemberpublications.com
Or
Email us at contact@maydecemberpublications.com

TW Brown is the author of the **Zomblog** series and the **Dead** series. He is deeply immersed in pursuing his dream of being a "full-time" writer while trying to balance the duties of husband, father, friend, and Border Collie owner. He keeps busy reading and editing the numerous submissions for a variety of upcoming anthologies and full-length titles for May December Publications. He has had short stories published by Pill Hill Press, Living Dead Press, and others. You can contact him at: twbrown@maydecemberpublications.com or visit his website at www.maydecemberpublications.com. You can follow him on twitter @maydecpub and on Facebook under Todd Brown, Author TW Brown, and also under May December Publications.

www.ingramcontent.com/pod-product-compliance
Lightning Source LLC
Chambersburg PA
CBHW060057150626
46556CB00017BA/1313